I0614786

# Copyright

Library and Archives Canada Cataloguing in Publication

Ritchings, Monty 1951 -

The Ascenders Return to Grace Book 2

paperback

Monty C. Ritchings

ISBN: 978-1-7388754-2-9-

# Table of Contents

# The Ascenders
# Return To Grace
# Book 2
## Monty Clayton Ritchings

"We do not inherit the earth from our ancestors,
We borrow it from our children."

# Chapter 1

Mike pondered the biggest question he had needed to answer in recent memory.... as he sat on the seat of his vintage Harley-Davidson motorcycle. It brought back so many memories to just sit there, recalling all the cold cases he had solved back so many years ago, hoping for some inspiration.

Today was a different world though, as he sat in front of the abandoned bar where he and Tomas had ousted a motorcycle gang that had taken the bar hostage as their clubhouse... at least until Tomas used it to show off his skill at using his positive energy to reframe bad situations.

Today was different as well in one other very significant way.... Mike was not just Mike! He was one of the first of a new breed of human beings. They were called Homo integratis. He was sitting in front of this abandoned bar because... Merle suggested it.

Who was Merle? She is his fully integrated female half. He and Merle shared the same body, sort of. Sometimes Mike looked like Mike as a guy and sometimes he found himself re-invented into a female (including her body) named Merle. They had learned to get along with each other. It took a while, but since they kind of had to travel everywhere together, they had little choice. During a break from being part of the team at the Matrix, they had learned how to talk with each other and conceded that since they share the same body, they had better learn to work together and like it!

Now, sitting on his motorcycle, Mike pondered, Merle pondered. She thought it would be helpful if they rode over to this old bar to reconnect with the energy to figure out where the leader of that gang had disappeared to.

Why might you ask?

Merle thought they might get some ideas from this man about how to create a cover. The bad man from whom they had rescued not one, not two, but three large groups of children that he had captured and intended to sell off into slavery was preparing to capture a fourth set. This time, he was going to do the job himself, since everyone else seemed so incapable of pulling off the jobs the way he wanted.

Three times they had relieved him of his property! All three times, his people had disappeared, never to be found again. The whole situation baffled the bad man, but he was determined that this mission was going to be done right this time. Soon his clients would forget about his past fumbles.

Merle felt that if they could find the leader of this gang, who supposedly knew this guy, might be of service to them. Or maybe, once they find him, he should get another dose of Tomas' amazing energy! No, that was not the way things worked for members of Homo integratis. Everything they took on, they completed with the highest of intentions, so they just needed to ensure that he will cooperate on his own.

As they continued to ponder, Merle drew the scene of the bikers wreaking havoc in the bar. Then she drew a picture of Tomas washing the bikers with golden light, the power of Universal Love.

Then, as Mike sat looking around, who did he see wandering up the street but the gang leader!

"Merle, you lovely creature, you did it again!" Mike laughed as he felt a kick in his side (from the inside). Then he heard a loud snicker from inside too as Merle looked out, transforming herself to the outside. She looked ravishing in her black leathers. Who wouldn't want to stop to chat with her, especially a former leader of a notorious motorcycle gang?

As he walked up, Merle noted as he came into view that he looked as much as a motorcycle gang leader as a chicken looked like a monkey! She knew it was him though because she could read his energy imprint. Even though his life had been transformed that fateful day, she knew it was him.

"Hello, Lindsay!" Merle smiled at him as he walked by.

Lindsay looked at her, shocked, as she addressed him, trying to figure out if he should know her.

Lindsay smiled (Who wouldn't be, looking at this beauty!), and then asked her, "How do you know my name, there beautiful?" He stood nearby on the sidewalk, not moving toward her, just waiting.

"I know a lot about you, Lindsay. Have you some time to chat with me? You might have some information I need." She replied.

"This is too weird," Lindsay muttered, more to himself than to Merle. "I was walking down a street not far from here going to meet some friends for coffee when I got the urge to walk over this way. Then I come walking along here and you are sitting here waiting for me. Don't you find that a little weird? I am sorry, you know my name, but I do not know yours... or what information I might have that you may need. Nice bike, by the way!"

"Life does have these moments, doesn't it?" she laughed at him, then reached out her hand to him. "My name is Merle. I apologize if this seems so unsettling to you. I am sure though that you have had other strange occurrences near here at some time."

Lindsay looked around and shrugged his shoulders. "Can't say I have had much to do with this area, but there have been some strange occurrences in my life."

"Let me help you recall, my friend," and with that, she projected some special energy into his hand as they connected. He bounced backward, like he had shaken hands with a bolt of lightning, landing on his back on the sidewalk.

"What did you do, Merle? I have felt nothing like that before," he replied as he picked himself up. "I do remember this area now! It's funny, until this moment, my mind would only go back a few years, then everything went fuzzy. I remember waking up one day knowing I had to go back to school, so I did. Now I am almost finished becoming a special education teacher."

Merle smiled at him, saying "You are now living your true destiny, Lindsay. You had a life before that was too far off base from what you were born to do. You might say friends of mine helped you find your way."

Lindsay smiled and said, "I am glad they did. I can now recall everything. It all came back, just like it was never gone. My childhood was really rough. I had to raise myself and I guess I did not do a very good job of it. I got into a lot of trouble when I was a kid, so it wasn't much of a stretch to become a member of a notorious motorcycle gang. I think they called me Dorf. It is a shortened version of my last name. I guess I could not be very notorious with a name like Lindsay, could I?"

"So what can I help you with, Merle?" he asked.

Merle explained without going into much detail about the mission she was on. She was going to rescue some children that were going to be kidnapped by a man who had worked with a local group of thugs. She was putting together the mission but needed more information about this man. They planned to offer their services to him.

"I can tell you lots about him, and I would love to be involved. This guy has to be stopped," he replied.

Almost on cue, they could hear the roaring of motorcycles racing toward them. Both Merle and Lindsay jumped from the noise, then stood waiting, looking up the street.

Seven vintage Harleys, all identical to the one Merle rested on, pulled up beside her. The leader stopped, pulling his bike up right beside her. He then stared at her for a moment and then laughed.

"Oh Goose, you scared us." Merle laughed. "This is Lindsay. He used to be the leader of a notorious motorcycle gang."

"Bad as us?" Goose said with a grin from ear to ear, looking at Lindsay.

Lindsay just stood there and stared, not sure what to do or say. These guys looked really tough, and he did not want to go back to that time in his life again for anything.

Merle looked at Lindsay, almost apologetically, then said to him, "Lindsay, meet Goose. You have a lot to learn. This was quite unexpected, but if you are willing, and have the time right now, you are going to get the ride of your life!"

Lindsay looked at Goose again, then at Merle, as he jumped on the back of Merle's motorcycle.

"I don't know what I am in for, but there is something about you, Merle, that I know I can trust, so let's go. Guess my friends will have to have their visit without me!" Lindsay laughed as they rode off with a roar.

"Wind Surfers, eh? Doesn't sound very notorious!" Lindsay said to Merle, pointing at the colors on the jackets of the other riders.

# Chapter 2

He was not sure what he had gotten himself into, but Lindsay knew deep inside he could deal with whatever developed. He was having fun. It had been a long time since he had ridden a motorcycle, especially in a gang.

Lindsay let himself become one with the feeling of being a biker again, as he rode along on the back of Merle's bike. He watched the other riders as they cruised. These guys seemed as if they had ridden these vintage Harleys for years. He knew this was no ordinary gang, as no real bikers he ever knew would make the effort to ride identical motorcycles, especially vintage black Harleys.

As he enjoyed the ride, he noticed that the colors on their jackets had changed. They now read Crool Dudes in a horseshoe shape with a fierce-looking red skull in the center. His mind melted.

It was not a long ride to the Matrix, but it became an eventful one for Lindsay. Things really made little sense; however, he was sure there would be explanations. As they parked in front of the Matrix, he turned to Goose saying, "Cool Bike, how long you been riding?"

Goose looked at his watch. He laughed as he said, "About an hour now."

Merle took Lindsay by the arm and led him inside the building, with the Crool Dudes laughing and fooling around not far behind. Lindsay looked out the window for one last look at the collection of vintage black Harleys, only to find Merle's bike sitting alone. Now he was feeling nervous!

Merle led him into the break room where she offered him a chair as she went to make them a drink. As she headed for the kitchen, she said, "Let's have some tea and snacks while we chat. I assure you that everything will make sense by the time you head off today."

It was fortunate that Lindsay felt safe with Merle because he was ready to run for the hills screaming for his mother! Nothing of this made sense at all, but he made himself sit. HIs safety mechanism was on high alert. He almost needed to staple himself to the chair.

Merle placed a nice big mug of sweet-smelling tea in front of him, then returned to the kitchen to bring in the plate of sweets. Lindsay took a little sip of the tea, not sure what he was being given. It tasted very different, but it seemed like his body craved whatever was in it, so he gulped it down as fast as he could. It was gone before Merle could even return with the goodies.

Lindsay closed his eyes. He felt as if he wanted to go to sleep, but his mind was sharp. He saw a brilliant light in front of him. As it became brighter, it moved closer to him. Finally, it took form, the form of a beautiful woman with long blond hair wearing a lavender gown.

The woman in his mind looked at him, saying, *"I am Rachel. I serve the Universal God that created this earth and all that exists. I invite you to join me in this moment of knowing yourself through the eyes of God."*

She then continued looking at Lindsay, remaining quiet to allow their connection to build. After a long pause, she said, *"Your truth is about to be revealed to you. This is your opportunity to serve mankind and the God of your heart in the highest order. If you choose to accept, it will change forever your life for your highest and best."*

She again remained silent, pouring her loving energy into his being. Slowly, she faded away until Lindsay sat staring at the beautiful golden light, feeling the best he had ever felt.

Sometime later, he opened his eyes. Merle sat across from him. She smiled as he opened his eyes. Neither said a word for the longest time. Lindsay looked around the room. It was so quiet and warm, the kind of warm one would feel nuzzling their mother when they were a babe. He felt so good, so safe. He had no memory of ever feeling this safe at any time in his entire life.

All of a sudden there was a clammer outside the door! It was as if a herd of bulls was stampeding along a narrow street in Pamplona during the running of the bulls!

The door crashed open and in poured seven young men and a tiny lady. This lady was so small she could easily be a butterfly if she wanted!

The eight of them grabbed drinks and treats, then joined Merle and Lindsay at the table. So much for peace, quiet, and tranquility!

Goose looked at Lindsay, smiling his Goose smile. Lindsay stared back at him, then finally Goose said, "So you liked our motorcycle gang, did you? That was super fun today!"

Lindsay, realizing that nothing was going to make sense today, laughed and let himself get into the moment, saying, "Yah, but you spelled Cruel wrong on your colors!"

"I couldn't decide if it should be 'cruel' or 'cool', so I combined them into a new word. Is that okay, Teach?"

Merle turned the meeting serious at that moment. She looked at Lindsay and said, "We would like you to help us. You have seen a few of our special skills. We need you to understand that we are not just ordinary folk asking for a helping hand. We serve our God through our Guardian Angel Rachel, who administers and leads this organization.

This is our home. We call it the Matrix. Every person who lives here has been blessed through Rachel to have the ability to act in ways that are beyond the normal concept of human ability. Everything you have experienced today is real, at least as real as reality is. As you have already seen, we can do so much more than most people... and so can you."

Merle then explained to Lindsay about the creation and purpose of the Matrix, saving the concept of the new species until last. She wanted to make sure that he was comfortable and on board with them before she reframed herself back into Mike.

"We have now successfully rescued three sets of kidnapped children from this man and his organization," Merle said. You are looking at the balance of group one with exception of Papillon, who came from group two. The other children chose to be adopted into families in the community, but they remain active members, and so do their adopted families.

We would like your help in rescuing group number four, the last group this man will collect for us. Will you consider leading us, Lindsay?"

As he sat there, a beautiful Golden Butterfly landed on his shoulder and sat in silence, gentling flapping its wings. He looked to the side, taking in the ravishing beauty of this gentle creature that had taken rest on his person.

There was no other choice than to say yes.

# Chapter 3

T here was still time before Lindsay was available to work with them, and the man had not completed his part of the job, so there was time for a different activity.

This time, it was Phoenix who suggested. "When we were playing at the beach where we learned that cool music, I thought I would go for a little tour on my own. I took myself for an aerial view of the local area. It was exciting seeing the ocean, the little town, and the mountains.

While I was flying over the town, I noticed a large campsite near the edge of town. I swooped down to have a look to see if they were playing music as well. When I got closer, I almost lost my concentration! The energy at the campsite was very low. People were milling around that had very confusing energy, like they had lost their connection with Source. The garbage and odor were almost unbearable!

I thought, what has happened to these people? What might have caused them to choose this lifestyle? What happened to the government that it has let its citizens live like this?

I propose that while we have time, let's see what we can do to help these people. I just can't seem to let go of the pictures in my mind."

Hummingbird, not one to speak up much, became agitated and started bouncing around. "Let's do it!" he got out between cartwheels and tilt-a-whirls. "Maybe we can play our music to help them!"

---

At first, no one in the camp noticed the group of young people gathered at the end of their park, as they were too immersed in whatever they were doing to make their lives work in their daily routines. Many of them were likely sleeping since having chosen to be a street person can tend to be a nocturnal affair.

The gang found a comfortable place where they could all just sit under a beautiful maple tree. The tree spread its branches as wide as it could to provide them both protection from the sun and to show off the beauty of the leaves it had created to celebrate summer.

They sat facing away from the camp as if their intent was to ignore that it existed, then pulled out their musical instruments. The music flowed through the air, wafting right into the camp. Each song was so beautiful, simple, and easy to absorb. It was simply hypnotic.

They played for quite a long time before the people in the camp took notice. The gang sent love in every note that flowed, hoping to entice the campers to embrace the music. However, that did not happen!

Several people from the camp came over to the musicians, alright! They had baseball bats, determined to be rid of these invaders! How dare they interfere in the sanctum of their privileged world!

They continued to play, facing away from the camp. They were aware of the angry people moving toward them, but they continued playing without changing their intention or the quality of the music.

"What do you mean interfering in our space?" one lady yelled at them. "We don't want your music and we sure don't want you interfering in our space, so go away!"

The music continued without a break, and so did the rapture from the campers. More and more of them gathered near the gang, but none ever attempted to interrupt the music.

It took a while, but soon a few of the campers sat on the ground nearby, not realizing that the music was providing food for more than their ears. For the first time in a long time, they found peace. As more and more of them took refuge on the ground near the musicians, the anger dissipated, and the weapons dropped.

At just the right moment, Hummingbird sprang up and started his crazy dancing. He kept playing his flute but became one with the music, like a Sufi in his hypnotic trance, as a Whirling Dervish. Some campers even laughed at him.

In the middle of all this, a huge angry man appeared right in front of the musicians. He was bent on destruction. This was his domain. These were his people, and no one interacted with them without his consent!

He started swinging a bat at the musicians. He came within striking distance, determined to do damage, spewing profanities like the gang had never heard. (Actually, they had never heard swearing, so they did not understand what he was saying!)

As he slashed his bat toward Phoenix's head, he got the shock of his life. Literally!

He poured all his strength into striking down at Phoenix, but each time he brought the bat down intending to do harm, the bat floated back up to his shoulder. He looked like a baseball player ready for the pitch.

After several attempts, he moved over and tried again to hit Raven... with the same result. Now, he was getting furious!

He had even more reason to get angry. His determination had turned into a comedy scene! The other campers began laughing at him! (It was comical to watch, although he did not see it that way!)

He turned away from the musicians and marched toward the campers. He had decided that if he could not take his anger out on the gang, he would take it out on his minions. They were his to do as he pleased, and today, some would be sorry for laughing at him!

As he approached the closest person, he prepared to strike, and strike hard. The person just sat there, looking up at him. He brought the bat down! This person was going to pay big time! But they didn't!

The bat did the same thing! As he brought it down, the energy of the swing diffused... and floated back to his shoulder!

He tried over and over, without success, until one woman looked at him and said, "Give it a rest, will you! Come sit down with me. I want to enjoy the music!"

When he sat down beside her, he fell over, with his head landing in her lap. He started bawling like a hungry baby! All that frustrated anger releasing as tears. She put her hand across his chest to cuddle him and let him cry.

Every member of the camp was soon sitting behind the gang. The music mesmerized them. It was so peaceful. Now was the time for the gang to go into action!

They all got up in a flash, turning to face the group, they ramped up the tempo. The music was like an Irish jig salsa. Who could sit around through that?

As if a light from heaven had struck them, all the campers, including the man who had threatened them, were up laughing and moving like crazy people to the beat of the music. The air of the camp turned on a dime at that moment... never to be the same!

As the music continued flowing and hugging them, the campers remembered who they were. They recalled life before they had slumped in desperation, unable or unwilling to carry their life's load. Thoughts of their families, their friends, all the people they had left behind before this part of their life had begun, filled their minds.

An ocean of tears flowed. A lonely cry, a cry of the soul, a soul that wanted to be fed, released them from their prisons.

Even though they were in a heightened emotional state, they continued to dance. As the dancing continued, the healing began. For the first time in a long time, some of them smiled... a genuine smile... a smile from their heart.

It was many hours later that it became quiet. The campers, exhausted, returned to their tents. They slept. They slept a sleep they had not enjoyed for a very long time. These people felt safe, an inner safety that can only express through knowing one's true self.

The gang returned home to their beds as well. It had been a long day. It was a very successful day... They were not done yet.

When the gang returned to the site a few days later, the campers had vanished. The people, the tents and equipment... gone. There was not even a speck of garbage on the ground! Even the grass had regrown. One would never have known that the camp had ever been there.

For the first time in a very long time, families were picnicking on the grass, children played on the swings, running around with not a care in the world. What a difference!

They decided that since they were there, they should sit and play some music and frolic around for themselves. Everything had worked out well, so why not a little me time!

They played some cool upbeat music, and of course, Hummingbird let loose. Papi and Tarita flew around doing loop-de-loops and dive bombs, and whatever else came into their beautiful butterfly minds. They all just let it go.

It took a while, but the picnickers did take notice of the musicians (how could they not?) and joined in the gaiety. The children let loose as they joined Hummingbird with his crazy dancing. They especially loved the butterflies showing off their flying skills!

The sound of the cheerful music spread through the air, reaching out to the homes in the area. The park filled as more and more families joined in the fun. Radiant faces were the only faces to be found for miles.

Now, how did the food trucks know to show up? I suspect Goose had something to do with that, since he loves to eat. The guys tease Goose, calling him the Food Truck Siren.

When things quietened down a bit, one local walked over to the gang and set sights on Merle. She walked right up, putting her hand out to her, and began. "I am so thankful that you brought your musicians to this park. For the last few days, we have been talking about the changes that have happened. We cannot explain what we saw. We know it resulted from your music though."

Merle shook her hand and replied, "Yes, it shocked us as well when we arrived back here today to find the park back to normal. Would you tell me what happened?"

The woman shook her head, bewildered. "We live right across from the park. We have had to endure these people for several years because the local government officials don't have any power to deal with these freeloaders.

Every time the police ordered them off the property, a couple of days later, they came back. After a couple of evictions, they returned and started breaking into our houses and our businesses and that big guy started taunting some neighbors. Everyone had become so afraid and so fed up, but no one knew what to do. We were stuck in a bad situation."

"We were fearful that they would return after you folks came and played the music. However, we know now that they will not be back. Would you like to know what happened between the time you were here before and today?" she laughed like she had just won the big prize in the lottery.

Before Merle could say anything, she launched right into her story. "When you folks left, they were all fast asleep. They slept until the following morning, not the next morning, but the next one. They made not one bit of noise the whole time.

When they did stir, they tippytoed around so they were no bother to anyone else. They all kind of sat around for a while, staring at each other like they had just woken up from a long dream. Then, after about an hour, some of them got up and started cleaning up, sorting things out. It looked like they were packing up!

It was going to be a big job for them to clean up and get everything organized, but a couple of hours later, cars started appearing. People were getting out of the cars and coming to help them. I couldn't stop watching! I was transfixed, trying to figure out what was going on.

As I watched the activities, I soon realized that the people in the cars were friends or relatives of the campers. Some of them, when they arrived, went searching through the camp. When they saw who they were looking for, they gave them a big hug like they had not seen them for a very long time. Nobody left the site, though, until they had packed everything up, even the garbage.

Just like a magic broom to finish the cleanup, a big truck came. Everyone pitched in to help load the truck with all the stuff that would have been left behind, and then it was like they had never been here at all!

The neighbors soon started coming out of their houses and walking into the park. At first, they were careful, watching for needles and such, but they soon relaxed, as they found nothing. All the campers seem to have been retrieved by their families! I have never seen such a thing."

She smiled; a smile that almost made her face explode at Merle. She then turned and walked back to her family.

# Chapter 4

"Okay! I am ready to get started on our new adventure!" Lindsay stated as he entered the break room at the Matrix. "Is there more of that delicious tea?"

This was perfect, Merle thought to herself. Once he has the tea, he will be more open, so I can transition into Mike. He needs to be able to work with both of us whenever we need. He needs to meet Tomas as well.

Tarita was sitting with Merle when Lindsay came in, so as soon as they saw him, she got up and headed for the hot drink dispensers. She looked at Lindsay and smiled, then greeted him. "I will get it for you Lindsay, just pull up a chair with Merle."

Tarita pretended to look around the drink section, then said, "Oh, I guess we have used up all the tea here. I will slip into the kitchen to get some."

As she stepped out of sight, she reached into her pocket and pulled out a packet of Destiny Tea, freshly manifested, then returned to make his tea.

"Here you go, Lindsay. It is nice to see you again," she said to him as she returned to sitting at the table.

In a blink of an eye, the tea did its magic. Lindsay closed his eyes and slid off into the ethers. He just relaxed and let go. He saw a beautiful lady floating in the air in front of him. There was just something about her that caused him to melt on the spot. For this woman, he would do anything. In each breath, he could just feel the goodness in her to the depths of his soul. He knew he could trust her.

Lindsay continued watching her smiling at him, then Rachel turned to everyone that sat at the table. In the next breath, he saw Mike and Tomas sitting with him.

At first, he was a little shaken, but he felt the goodness in her eyes, so he relaxed again. Then he looked again and saw Tarita and Merle. This continued back and forth, back and forth until he began laughing so hard, especially as he saw Merle sitting with a beautiful Golden Butterfly.

When Rachel had finished the demonstration, she spoke. "I *am Rachel. I serve the Universal God that created this earth and all that exists. I invite you to join me in this moment of knowing yourself through the eyes of God.*"

Lindsay looked lovingly back at her, recognizing her like an old friend, then took Rachel's hand. He rose from the chair, floating into the air, and flew with her. In only a second, he was standing looking at a person who he thought might be a distant relative. This person smiled, then raised their hand to point back behind Lindsay. Lindsay turned around to look. His life purpose flashed before his eyes, and he knew.

Sometime later, he opened his eyes to see Mike and Tomas sitting in the same place where Merle and Tarita had been sitting. He sat for a while, just to enjoy the feeling of his journey for as long as he could. When he looked at them again, Merle and Tarita were there. He laughed, looking at Tarita, then said, "I suppose you are going to become a Golden Butterfly now!"

With that, there was a Golden Butterfly perched on his arm. He looked at her through his new eyes. He was okay! This was the beginning of his new life. He knew it was going to be somewhat different than he had thought earlier, but now he had a Golden Butterfly for a friend. Who could ask for more?

When he was present enough to take part in a conversation, Mike brought him food to help him get grounded. Tomas grabbed him a cup of hot coffee, then they waited for Lindsay to start.

"I am feeling so humbled and so honored by what has happened to me since I have become associated with you folks. My life purpose seems to be so much clearer, and I feel connected with myself rather than flipping about scattered like I am used to. Now, I am ready to help you and to be a servant of Rachel and Universal Source.

While I was finishing my schooling, I contacted this guy you have on your radar. I offered to provide the manpower to help him complete his task. He was wary at first, wanting to know what had happened to me. He told me he had come to the pub, but no one could find any trace of me.

It seemed odd to him I should just show up now when I was looking for some help. Not a very trusting person! He told me others had already messed with him three times, so he wanted to make sure that the right people were going to help him get this job brought to a successful conclusion.

I told him that the police arrested our entire gang soon after they had arrested the group that had held the first group of children. We were all taken to a high-security prison, so secure that they even made our files inaccessible. They let us out a short time ago since they deemed us to no longer be a threat to society.

I will reach out to him again when we are ready, and see where he is at with the selection process," he said as he concluded his report.

Mike looked at him with a smile on his face and said, "This is super, Lindsay. You have already provided valuable information to help us move forward. Now what we have to do is start planning."

"Yes, this guy is going to be a bit skittish, so we need to either make ourselves fit right in as his co-conspirators. We need to stand nearby and jump in when he needs us," Tomas added to the conversation.

"How do you keep tabs on him?" asked Lindsay.

As fast as he could ask, Merle reappeared. "Take my hand," she said to him.

The next thing Lindsay knew, he was standing in a coffee shop watching the man having a discussion with some seedy-looking characters.

Lindsay looked down at himself as they stood there, then at Merle, whispered, "Cool outfits! I always wanted to dress up like a spy!"

Merle giggled and replied, "Goose told me we always have to look the part!"

They purchased drinks and sat close enough to listen to the conversation going on at the table where the man sat. They were speaking a language Lindsay did not understand, but of course, Merle did. When he went to say something, Merle raised her hand to quieten him so she could hear better.

After a few minutes, the men finished their meeting, got up, and left. So then Merle filled Lindsay in with the details.

"These three men are some bad dudes, at least they used to be. He wants them to prepare the site where they will hold the children after they capture them. It is on a remote island. Because he is being so cautious, he did not even name the island.

He is still looking for people to go with him to kidnap the children, so we still have a chance."

Lindsay relaxed, then asked her, "What do you mean, they used to be bad dudes?"

Merle smiled that smile that asks why one asks the obvious, then said, "I just put a gentle little note in their minds to remind them who they are in truth. Not enough to make them give up their criminal activities, but enough that when we need them to, they will be compliant."

"Let's head back to the Matrix," Merle said, and with that, she took his hand, and voila, they were sitting in the break room at the Matrix.

The room was getting quite full now as the Wind Surfers, or should I say, The Crool Dudes, had joined them. It was easy to see that the conversation had been very light in the room until Merle and Lindsay reappeared. Everyone got a kick out of their spy costumes. Merle had forgotten that part of returning, so they got up and paraded the outfits to the entire gang.

As everyone continued laughing and frolicking, Mike reappeared, and at that same moment, Rachel presented herself, so they all became quiet.

She smiled her ever radiant smile, then began, "*He is getting closer to activating his plan, but he is waiting for the war to do its part. The fighting has slowed down somewhat, so he has more time than he had hoped. It is time for you to establish yourselves at a base near him, so he knows you are available. Before you physically station yourself there though, I have a practice run for you to do, so that Lindsay is more than ready.*"

# Chapter 5

It did not upset Papi that they did not include her in the motorcycle ride. Although she loved riding on motorcycles, she had finally learned that this world was not just about her. She knew she had important jobs to do and that the boys sometimes had to do things without her.

She also knew that when Goose got back from this mission, he would be happy to take her for a nice, long ride. It was a challenge for her, though. She was so tiny that her legs could only just straddle the seat of the bike, never mind touch her feet on the pedals.

Sometimes she consoled herself by saying under her breath that she was the lucky one because they could not be a Golden Butterfly!

However, she was beside herself with happiness when she looked out the window of the Matrix and saw the eight of them riding up on their identical Harleys.

While they were away, Papi worked with Tarita. Tarita had some very special skills she wanted to teach her amazing student, courtesy of Rachel.

They were to be special spies for the Matrix. This was the result of Papi doing such a great job finding the children that were being transported into slavery on a boat a few years ago.

It was pretty obvious this little butterfly was cut out for the world of espionage!

She had also matured enough now that she was now a master intuitive, connected in harmony with the Cosmic. Now Universal

Love empowered her instead of the old way when she operated in anger. This change had given her so much extra power, she forgot the anger that had been her motivator for so many years.

Papi knew bits and pieces of what was happening around the Matrix, but they had not briefed her in full. She was okay with the situation though. She felt content as she practiced becoming a better butterfly. She was so proud of herself, and of Tarita as well. They could both remain in butterfly for as long as they needed, but could pop back to being human in an instant. There was no doubt that this skill would have its advantages along the way. Then, as she thought about it, she realized that being able to go into butterfly at her convenience might even be more important in case she needed to skedaddle if things went awry!

Papi had also been working every day with the third group of children. These people were just as amazing as the first two groups had been. Each one of them had already shown their abilities to keep up, and in some ways, surpass the capabilities of the Wind Surfers. None of them would be adopted out, as they felt their unique offerings would serve little purpose in the real world.

None of the third group had shown any signs of being members of Homo integratis. However, there was a marked difference between the Wind Surfers and Mike and Tomas, who were the originals. One could only observe. The answer would soon reveal itself.

This could mean two things. First, there were only Homo Sapiens in the group, or second, they had progressed to a whole new level of development again. Papi suspected the second was more likely since their skill level in anything they tried was beyond normal Homo Sapien capacity. Only time would tell!

The time they played Capture The Flag against the Wind Surfers only went to show they had an immeasurable capacity to work with Source in ways Homo Sapiens could not even dream.

Papi was pretty careful about becoming a butterfly in front of them, but she thought they already knew about her abilities. She enjoyed being special, so she was not looking to share that little bit of limelight, at least not yet.

They could already teleport themselves, some of them could leap high into the air and do acrobatics, and they all could read minds. That was a pretty good start! They were learning more and more skills every day. Sometimes, they even came up with some on their own!

As the Crool Dudes parked their bikes, the third group headed out to greet them in their own special way. They formed a circle around the bikers by locking hands together, then closed their eyes and visualized the bikers levitating into the air. They were pretty good at it, except their visualizations went a little wonky when the motorcycles rose, but the men did not!

The Crool Dudes watched in amazement as their bikes formed a circle above them. The bikes revved their own engines and cat-walked, showing off to each other.

That was about the time the men headed for the safety of the building. They tried to sneak out, though, so as not to disturb the third group's visualization. After all, they did not want the bikes to come crashing down.

Their stepping out broke the concentration, though, and the bikes started falling to the ground. Well, at least for a second! As we have now come to expect, the bikes became like black feathers floating back into their parking spots.

The men came back out when it was safe. They were laughing their heads off as they re-entered the parking lot. After a lot of backslapping, the members of the third group agreed it was a great trick and very entertaining, but they also realized they had really messed up that visualization!

The next day, they called everyone into the yoga room for a meeting right after breakfast. Beth and Sheila had a major announcement to make, so everyone needed to be there.

It was Beth that got the meeting going. This must be the news everyone has been waiting for... and it was!

"Today is the official start of training for a secret mission," Beth said. "We are going to help capture some more war children."

Sheila jumped in at that spot. "No, we have not gone to the other side! We are just going to pretend that we have."

Sheila turned to Beth, signaling her to continue. "The man who was responsible for your being here today is planning to enter a country where there is a terrible war going on. His intention is to capture young children and sell them into slavery, just like he tried to do with all of you."

One could see the emotion on each of the children's faces. Even though they had worked through the emotional trauma of their childhood, it still left memories that gave them the incentive to help prevent any other child from enduring what they had.

Even though they felt upset, they remained quiet, waiting for Beth to go on.

"Now that Lindsay has joined us, we have created some plans of our own. Lindsay, pretending he is his old persona, has convinced the man that he and his gang have the capabilities to assist him to complete the job and get these children to their new homes, wherever that might be."

"Lindsay will lead the (and she laughed) Crool Dudes into war. Mike and Tomas will work ahead of Lindsay's group to ensure that as many children as possible get captured without suffering too much."

"Papi and the third group will also be nearby. We have arranged for a circus to be in a town near where the war is raging for the entire duration of this project. You folks are joining the circus!"

"If anyone needs extra or special help during the mission, you (she pointed to the new circus act members) will be pressed into service. Your special skills may come in handy!"

Sheila then said, "This is the biggest project we have ever undertaken. There is a lot of planning and training to be completed before you all journey over there. We need everyone to be 100% on board. No independent acting, just teamwork, and commitment.

We will complete our morning exercises as usual, then after lunch, we will begin the planning. There will be opportunity for everyone to contribute ideas. Because there are so many people involved, for the start, all ideas are to be submitted in written form, so Mike and Tomas can review them. Once we are farther down the road in the planning, you will still be able to offer ideas and concerns during meetings, but for now, please just write them down."

On that note, Beth and Sheila became quiet. Everyone knew what that meant. They closed their eyes and, sure enough, Rachel appeared.

*"Good morning all! This is an auspicious occasion. It is so important that every one of you takes your full place in this operation. The lives of many youngsters sit in your capable hands. We need these children to take their rightful place here at the Matrix, so we can help them heal first, and then, to expand our army to support the desires of the Beloved.*

*To speed up the preparation process, I am increasing the intensity of the power in everyone. This will support you in completing any tasks we assign you. As well they will help in stretching your abilities to do even more amazing techniques you might now not even be aware of possessing at present.*

*Each of you, although I am sure you will each enjoy this newfound energy, must treat this gift as a sacred covenant you make with Source. There will be an opportunity in this project for each of you to choose between selflessness and selfishness. Let your true colors shine through!"*

And with that, Rachel positioned her hands in prayer position in front of her chest, then nodded her head and disappeared. Not a breath could be heard in the room.

# Chapter 6

"Let's go do some mountain climbing while Mike and Tomas are planning," suggested Goose. "That will give us an excellent opportunity to test out our new energy!"

Songbird tweeted back "I have never done mountain climbing. Won't it look funny to the mountain climbing club if we accidentally become birds or such?"

Then Raven added, "Since we have this extra energy, and after all we saw when we played Capture the Flag, I think we are safe to do whatever we need without the guys from the club being involved. In fact, maybe we will be more comfortable as we can do what we need."

"Which is the thing we would do in any situation once we get on the project!" added Goose, turning to Papi, smiling. "Are you going to join us, Papi?"

"I will be first to the top," she laughed.

"Should we invite the third group?" asked Raven.

So it was set. The preparations were made, and the entourage was off to the hills. With tents, equipment, and enough food for four days, the bus they hired was chock full when it arrived at their camping site.

The bus driver was left scratching his head as he headed back to town, trying to figure out how the bus got unloaded so fast!

Before they went for an easy hike, they decided to just relax for a bit and get settled in. This little break would let them take in and enjoy the fresh air and beautiful scenery. It was nice to just do something that did not require managing other people for once.

As they relaxed, there was a loud crash in the bush near them that put everyone on edge. Then another crash. Something was working its way toward them, and it sounded angry!

They all focused on their breaths. They knew they were safe, so they just waited for who or whatever was making the noise to appear before them.

Before long, a huge black bear entered their camp. As she entered, she saw the people and stood up on her hind legs. She sniffed the air, then let out a loud roar. She was not happy because they were camping near her den. She was here to protect her new cubs.

Phoenix transitioned right away into a male black bear right in front of her. That was not a very smart thing to do! The transition shocked her, to say the least! Male bears have nothing to do with raising their young, so she put the run on this even more unwanted invader.

Phoenix galloped off into the forest away from the now very angry bear, going far enough that he could transition back into human without her seeing. That was definitely a whoopsy moment!

When he returned to camp, he sat down trying to be invisible, waiting for someone else to have a brilliant idea.

Raven then tried to talk to her in bear language by telepathy, but black bears are not good communicators at the best of times, so that did not work either. Besides, she was still feeling angry at these invaders, so why would she want to chat? Would they invite her for tea and berries next?

The bear settled back onto its fours after a beautiful Golden Butterfly landed on its nose. How could anyone, including a protective mother bear, remain angry when a butterfly, especially a beautiful Golden Butterfly perched itself on its nose?

Papi remained sitting on the bear's nose, flapping her wings and, unbeknownst to the bear, staring into its eyes, projecting loving energy into her.

Soon, the bear became very docile and friendly. In fact, she turned around and trotted off back into the forest. They all relaxed, relieved that the little event was over!!

"Phew, that was a learning experience!" Phoenix laughed. "I guess I should know more about who I am trying to appease before I jump into action."

Everyone laughed and laughed, slapping Phoenix on the back.

Things were just getting back to normal when they heard a bunch of crashing again from the same area as before. They all just sat down and watched in the direction of the noise.

The mother bear reappeared before them again... with Papi still riding on her nose! And... behind her were two almost newborn cubs trailing behind!

She had come back to show off her cubs!

The cubs came right into the camp. They were not afraid of these others; they just saw play friends. Right away, several of the third group transitioned themselves into bear cubs and joined into some fun frolicking about. They ran off into the forest with Mother bear's children, jumping into the nearby stream to splash around, walking on fallen trees, and climbing trees right to the top. All kinds of little bear fun!

In the meantime, Mother Bear, with Papi still on her nose, sauntered down to the stream. She sat there looking at the water for a while, and, at just the right time, she reached in and grabbed a huge salmon. Throwing the salmon with a strong toss onto the rocks on the shore, it lay quiet, like it was sleeping.

She continued reaching in until she had caught enough fish for the entire camp to enjoy dinner that night!

When she had finished fishing, she turned to the campers with an appreciative look, then lowered her head to the fish. She remained in that position until Raven realized she was giving thanks to the fish for giving up their lives so they could all eat.

"She is waiting for us to join her in giving thanks, everyone. Come on, let's make a circle with her!" Raven shouted.

So they all gathered on the beach and made the best circle they could to give thanks together. It was a rocky beach, so it was difficult to assemble into a circle, but they managed it. The mother bear even let two of them put their hands on her back so they could all connect.

After they gave thanks, they all joined in to carry the fish back to camp. Supper was going to be a most special meal tonight.

As they had finished the task, the young cubs returned with their new friends. Mother bear then collected them up, and set off to return to her den. All three walked to the edge of the camp, then turning toward the campers, stood up, gave huge bear smiles, and waved to their new friends.

"Well, that was a good start to our current adventure! Let's have some lunch after we get these wonderful fish put away, then head off for a little hike," Condor suggested.

So, not long later, the first hike was on. This area was a park, so it had plenty of trails to wander along. Since Songbird was new to the hiking game, they thought doing a somewhat flat walk would let him test his new equipment. The trail they selected had a fair climbing wall a few miles into it, so if they wanted, they could do some scaling as well.

Goose walked along with Songbird. He wanted to brief him on some rules for hiking and climbing that were specific to their group.

"First thing you need to know and agree to practice is no cheating. The object of these activities is to remain in your human form unless you deem the situation to be an emergency, like falling off a cliff. We prefer that you try your level best to resolve the issue in human form. You will need that skill when we get to the real project of rescuing the children," he said.

"What is the point of being able to transform into a bird if I have to use my human form to complete a task that can be dangerous and take many hours when I can do the entire job in seconds in bird form?" Songbird asked.

"The point of these activities is to help each of us to be the best human participants. How much trust or credibility do you think the man we are going to work for will give you if you turn into a bird whenever things get tough? Besides, it is an aspect of being Homo integratis that sets us aside from regular humans from what I have seen. We perform in the highest manner possible in any event. Turning yourself into a bird without justification is not in your highest interest. You might want to have a chat with Papi about that subject. She struggled with that for years!" Goose concluded.

It was good that the trail was pretty long since there were so many people hiking in this group. Almost forty people had joined in for the trip! The third group were good sports, so things went along with no problems for much of the journey.

When they reached the climbing bluff, they all found a place to sit. It was tough to find enough seating because they were in a deep forest, but they managed it.

This was Condor's passion, to be hanging around on the edges of cliffs. All he wanted to do right now was to get his gear on and get up that bluff. Being a sensible sort of person, he knew he needed to temper his emotions though, so the newcomers could get in on the excitement. Condor was also a fanatic for safety, so he took on the job of showing the newbies how to get into their gear. He showed them how to make sure it was safe, and of course, how to use it to climb the bluff.

The bluff was about one-quarter mile long, with most of it climbable. This meant there was plenty of room for several of them to get on the face at one time, without interfering with the others.

The challenge was that there were thirty of them, with only the seven Wind Surfers who were experienced climbers. It took quite a long time for everyone to have a turn under a watchful eye.

Like everything each of them took on, they were pros in no time. It is amazing what a person can do when they have a positive mind and are open to learning something new.

For the Wind Surfers, there was no fear since they were all experienced climbers. It was much easier for them to do some risky moves in this sport. However, the third group, although they had not shown themselves to be able to transform themselves yet, were all very good at overcoming gravity. That is an excellent skill to have in your pocket when climbing, or in their case, hanging off the faces of mountains.

Once they had a good understanding of how to do rock face climbing, they each selected a spot on the face to do a solo climb. The Wind Surfers all stayed on the ground so they could watch how each climber fared. Not only were they looking for their level of competence, but they were also watching to make sure they obeyed the first rule- Stay Human!

---

That evening, they enjoyed the wonderful salmon Mother Bear had caught for them, along with some edible mushrooms from the forest and a salad made from plants that grow in the local area. What a treat!

Once they had finished the cleanup, as one would expect of this group, the music broke out. This was going to be a special night since they had never played music in such a serene setting before. Nobody to placate, just plain enjoyment.

It did not take long before they had an audience. Mother Bear strolled right into the camp and parked herself and her cubs right by the campfire. There was that magical bear smile again!

And if you think that Mother Bear and her family were alone in the audience, guess again! It was not long before other creatures were stirring in the woods nearby. It was not long until the music was complemented by wolf calls, bird calls and even the odd moose added their own bit in! What a great evening!

By the third day, everyone was running up and down the climbing bluff like it was flat, so Goose suggested to the third group that since they were going to be joining a circus when the project began, they should practice some interesting jumps and leaps that they might use in their acts.

Well! It was like a tornado had been turned loose in the area! The place looked like it was full of Mexican Jumping Beans! The gang had to move into the edge of the forest just to ensure they did not get landed on by someone jumping off the cliff.

Papi joined in, too. She was not going to waste one minute standing on the ground when there was a hill to be conquered. If there hadn't been so much noise created by the others, one could have heard her tiny little laughs as she played on her hill. She got so excited at one point that she forgot the first rule. Right in front of the third group, she transformed into her butterfly. Unlike when Mother Bear was introducing herself, she didn't go off somewhere out of sight. Oops!

The third group all saw her do it. In the shake of a grasshopper's tail, the place looked like a lepidopterarium! (How is that for a word!) Every inch of the wall became a butterfly house!

Papi looked around in complete shock. At first, she was annoyed because now she and Tarita had to share the luxury of being the only butterflies with the newbies, but then she remembered what Rachel had told her. Once she regained her composure, she laughed and flew off to play with her new butterfly friends.

Way too soon, the fourth afternoon arrived, and so did the bus to take them back to the Matrix. The bus driver had decided before he arrived he was going to watch closely from outside the bus. He was determined to see if he could figure out how they had unloaded the bus so quickly. However, when he arrived at the campsite and saw who was seeing off the group, he decided to just stay in his seat! (I bet he had some stories to tell when he got back to the depot!)

The gang was safe though, since no one was likely going to believe that a family of bears, a pack of wolves, and a lonely moose would be standing by to see their friends off anyway, never mind all the birds chirping!

# Chapter 7

T he time had come for them to begin assembling themselves for the big project. Everyone was giddy from the excitement. Songbird and Hummingbird kept flapping all over the place, driving everyone crazy!

Mike and Tomas had already headed over to survey the area. Lindsay needed to go next because he was the only one who still needed to fly the old-fashioned way. He needed to meet up with the man on his own anyway and begin laying out the plans with him, and of course, earning his trust.

Lindsay was feeling nervous about taking on this job as he knew how important it was for him to pull off this role. He had never been an actor before, but he did recall enough of his old life to engage that part of his old personality. He also did not like having to become so scruffy looking again, either.

However, on to bigger and better things!

They fit Lindsay with a device that allowed him to connect directly with Mike in case of an emergency. Other than that, he was on his own. Not having all the tools the others had, he had to rely on old-fashioned wit and intelligence. This would be a genuine test for him as things took shape.

He took a room in an old, rundown hotel in the area where the man had told him he would run the operation from. He got himself settled in, then he called him to set up an appointment.

"I am here and ready to begin," he said to the man as he answered his phone.

The man gave him directions where to meet him that afternoon. The project was now officially under way.

"How many helpers are you bringing, and when will they be here?" the man asked almost as soon as Lindsay sat down.

"Seven," he replied. They will be here tomorrow. "I wanted to meet with you first to get things organized before we started giving them marching orders."

So all afternoon, they sat and discussed the plans. The man threw in a couple of twisters to test Lindsay. At first, it shocked Lindsay, but when he realized the man was testing him, he went with it.

By nightfall, the plans were complete. As soon as his underlings 'appeared' (that was the man's word!) they would head off to the edge of the fighting.

Lindsay was really feeling nervous that evening. He could hardly even eat his dinner. This was the biggest and most important thing he had ever done, and he didn't want to mess it up.

He decided he would sit quietly in the chair in his room and try to make himself feel better by focusing on his breathing. Shortly after he began, Rachel appeared before him.

"*Dearest Lindsay, the time has now come for you to shine. I want you to know that I am here with you to support you in every step you take. Although this requires your human side to be in charge of your part in this project, you must listen to your higher side through your intuition. This man works alone, even if you and the Wind Surfers are with him, so you need to stay ahead of him. Watch the others as they will automatically know his mind, so go with their responses. The key to your success is to take the time to sit and focus on your breath when you have the opportunity. I cannot overstate the importance of this action for you,*" Rachel affirmed, smiling as she faded away.

Lindsay stayed in the chair for a long time, focusing on his breath, observing the pictures that came up on the screen of his mind. He realized that the man had intentionally set a trap for him and his gang so that he could test their allegiance to him. They needed to be on their toes around this guy!

---

After Lindsay had finished breakfast the next morning, he returned to his room. It was a very full room when he opened the door. All the Wind Surfers were huddled into it.

"We really should have gotten you a bigger room!" Raven laughed as Lindsay walked in.

Lindsay laughed and retorted, "yes, it is too bad the Hilton was full. This was all I could get on short notice!"

After a few minutes of kibitzing around, they all got serious. Lindsay led the discussion by updating them about the session with the man on the previous day, and about his meeting with Rachel last night.

"Rachel said to be careful around this man, that he was not to be trusted. She even said that he was planning a trap for us just to test our loyalty, so please be ready."

Lindsay picked up his phone and called the man. He told them to head over to an abandoned mill a few blocks from where he had met with Lindsay the day before. He would meet them there. When questioned about the meeting place, he got a little gruff and told them it was secluded. He did not want to be seen with them at a coffee shop.

"We can walk over there. It's only a few blocks," Lindsay said. "We had better get ourselves prepared for anything with this guy."

Goose sat down rather than getting his coat on. Everyone turned to look at him, then following suit sat down too. "Let's connect with Source while we have a minute. I also want to check in with the

Third group and make sure they made it to their destination. We need them close by, just in case."

---

The man was waiting at the mill site when they arrived. He was visibly angry because they had taken longer than he had expected. Several of the gang wanted to give him a little softening, but they knew better than to mess with him until the project was over. They had never really had to deal with this level of negative energy for a long period before, so it was a little discomforting.

"Let's go inside," he pointed toward a large freight door. As they walked in, he made sure he steered them from behind. After exploring the mill for several minutes, he guided them into an old beehive burner out back. As soon as everyone except himself was inside, he stopped... an enormous door came slamming down, sealing the gang inside the burner.

Outside the container, the gang could hear the laughing voices of several people. He had set a trap for them. It did not worry them, though. After all, it was just an old metal beehive burner.

However, as they looked around, they realized that this was not just an old beehive burner at all! The man had really planned this out to ensure they were stuck!

He had completely locked them into a metal box that appeared to have no openings. It was airtight!

They all sat down on the ground, finding as comfortable a position as possible, then started doing positive breathing to connect with Source.

"What the heck?" said Condor. "I can't seem to go to Source. There is something in the way blocking me!"

The others all replied that they were having the same issue. This had never happened before. Immediately, they became nervous, as they were now out of the huge comfort zone they knew.

Being masters of self-management, they calmed themselves down, recalling that Rachel had told them they would have to be able to deal with some issues using their human skills.

"Let's have a good look around, so we know what the complete challenge is. We need to figure out if he is just testing us or has he really set a trap to get us out of the way." Lindsay offered.

They soon realized that they were prisoners in a hinged metal box with only the dirt floor of the burner not sealed. They did not understand why they could not project out, but if they were patient, they likely would figure it out.

"My sense is that he is testing us. We have no normal way out of here. I think we should be patient for a while. We know we are safe, so let's sit tight and let the situation play out," suggested Goose.

"Let's play some music while we wait," suggested Hummingbird. "At least we can entertain ourselves until they release us."

As soon as he said it, there was a consensus, determining that was a bad idea. "If he comes back and we are playing music, he will probably question his decision about working with us. First, he will wonder how did we get the musical instruments, and second, how are we supposed to pull off being tough gangsters if we turn ourselves into metaphysical musicians?"

"Let's sit quietly for a while. I doubt he will just leave us here, so we need to be patient," said Lindsay.

Finally, a few hours later, they heard some creaking and groaning coming from the metal walls as they lifted the door back up to the top of the burner. It had been a test.

As the man walked into the burner, he laughed, and said, "Thought I would give you a little test to see what you are made of! We are heading into a dangerous area where there is no room for scaredy-cats."

Just for effect, each of the members grumbled out loud about being confined as they were getting themselves up and ready to leave. Having passed that test, they wondered what would happen next.

Sometimes, there is not much time between a question and an answer as the answer launched itself at them almost as they regained their freedom. Now the problem!

They could not use their metaphysical skills (really) against the horde of tough guys coming at them, but they could not stand there and let themselves get beaten up! What to do?

Sneaky time! Remember! One can always be what they choose when they remember that they already know how!

Those invaders were flat on the ground in only minutes as the gang reached inside their minds and pulled out their Inner Ninja!

It was a little difficult making all the martial arts moves while dressed as bikers, but they pulled it off with the desired result laying on the floor in a big heap.

The man looked upon the entire event with complete admiration and said, "Let's go get some lunch. I have worked up quite an appetite this morning!"

---

They all walked over a few blocks to an old restaurant that served set meals. As the man walked in, he motioned to all the men to sit at a large table while he got the food ordered. He stayed there during the complete preparations process, which seemed kind of odd to them, so they watched him from the corner of their eyes.

"Scan your meal before you eat. I just saw him take his plate from a different place than ours. There might be another trick up his sleeve." Goose said to the others in a quiet warning.

Sure enough, when the food arrived, they each checked out their meals and discovered that there was foreign material in their mashed potatoes. The rest seemed okay, though, so when they dug in to eat, it surprised the man when none of them touched the tainted food.

"You guys don't like potatoes?" he asked.

Condor laughed and replied, "We all have Irish in our heritage. We are still trying to get over the great potato famine!"

The man looked at the group with a completely stunned look on his face. Quietly he cursed, "Foiled again!"

Once lunch was over, he excused himself, saying that he would be in touch in the next day to prepare for travel to the site where they would go hunting.

Raven sauntered over to the cook, complimented him on the meal, and gave him thanks for providing for them. He then asked the cook if he saw the man put anything in the food. The cook reached into the cupboard and pulled out a bottle of laxatives.

"Well, I am glad we got the jump on him for that one! Wouldn't that make our day, all of us trying to get to the one toilet in Lindsay's room had we eaten those potatoes," Raven laughed.

"We may be working on this project as normal humans, but I will say that I am really thankful for the training I have received! I can think of other ways I would rather spend the rest of the day," laughed Condor.

"Speaking of the rest of the day," jumped in Lindsay. "We need to get ourselves prepared for the next step, and you guys need a place to stay. By the way, where did you guys sleep last night?"

They all just give him the look, followed by a sarcastic laugh in unison.

"Is it a busy freeway on your commute?" Lindsay laughed at them with a slight tinge of jealousy.

Turning serious, Goose turned to Lindsay, saying, "I think you should do some detective work around here and try to get the jump on this guy and his antics. I sure do not want to continue having to expect him to test us more. We are going to sleep in our own beds tonight, back at the Matrix after we get back to your room, so we can prepare ourselves completely. It is time for the fun to begin!

I am going to get Papi to drop by to help you this afternoon. She is an excellent spy, and she can keep an eye on you in case you run into any problems. She is not far away, and she will be looking to get away from the third group for a while. Even she tires of their high-energy antics sometimes!"

"How can I get a bead on the man so I can observe him discretely?" asked Lindsay.

Before he had even completed the question, Papi was sitting on his shoulder, flapping her little wings to say hello.

"There is your answer, Lindsay. Just let her lead you," said Goose as they each disappeared. To Lindsay, their disappearance was almost like popping bubbles from a soap dispenser. Six little pops and they were gone!

Quickly Papi transformed herself so they could discuss what Lindsay wanted to know. She sat quietly and focused, feeling for the man's energy. It only took her a couple of minutes to locate him.

"He is not far from here," she said. "He appears to be in a building. He is speaking with some others. Do you want me to guide you there or should I flip on over and see what I can find out, then report back to you?"

"How about if I walk part of the way with you? I will stay out of the way, then you can do our stuff, my little spy!"

And with a little laugh, Papi transformed herself back, and they were off. She led Lindsay on a little jagged tour of the neighborhood, but found the man right away, almost too fast, as Lindsay had to jump into an alley to prevent him from noticing him in the window of the building he was in.

Papi flitted away, looking for an opening that would allow herself into the building and the room the man was in. As luck would have it, a lady opened the door to come out of the building and Papi was right there.

"The first step," she thought. "Now to find the room and get in so I can hear them without them seeing me."

Suddenly, she got the strongest urge to get out of sight. She leaped right up to the ceiling of the hallway and hid as best as she could in a corner. Out came the man with another man right in front of her!

As they were talking, they entered the street right where Lindsay had been standing a minute before. Papi followed them, trying to listen in while she hunted for Lindsay to ensure he was out of the way. She saw him hiding behind a large garbage container, so she turned toward him and did a swoop to show him she had seen him. She turned and followed the men.

"These guys are skilled at their game, let me tell you," he said to the other man. "I tried three times to outsmart them, but they got me each time."

"I would be really careful with these guys. They seem to have some tricks of their own," the other man replied. "These are not your normal everyday hoods if they can beat you at your own game."

"I agree, but we need to get going on catching these children. My customers have been waiting for a very long time. I have the island all ready to store them until we can ship them, and I have gone overboard on providing protection so no one can sneak off with them. I am determined I am going to win this time, no matter what I have to do!"

The two men parted at that point, letting Papi return to find Lindsay waiting for her. Once she had reported what she had heard, Lindsay thanked her, heading off to his hotel room.

When he entered his room, Mike and Tomas were sitting in the room, waiting for him. Lindsay shook his head in amazement as he came over and sat down with them.

"This sure is a busy room!" he laughed. "I just left Papi to go back to the circus."

"Yes, we were watching. Glad things worked out well. Papi is going to be a great asset for this project, as you now see," said Mike.

"Let's spend some time preparing for what is ahead. We have already done a tour of the area, so now we need to fill you in, so you and the boys can be better prepared."

# Chapter 8

If there ever was a place on this planet that was a natural home to the third group, it was in a circus!

Yay for the third group!! They now had found a place where they could play, and play, and play. The other significant thing about it was that the people who came to watch did not realize it was not normal for people to jump over three feet up in the air. These guys could jump twenty feet, no problem!

Could you imagine if they had taken up basketball instead?

When they arrived, the man that ran the circus was not sure what he had gotten himself into. However, he was used to strange characters, and his business sure could use a boost.

"I am really glad to have you people on board with me. Getting amazing attractions for a circus is an ongoing challenge, especially since the bearded lady molted! I sure hope you have some wonderful tricks up your sleeves," he said to the third group members.

All the members giggled under their breath as they thought to themselves. "Silly man, we are all wearing t-shirts. We do not have sleeves."

After they got themselves settled in, the owner brought them to the main tent. He did not know what to expect, so he decided he would just turn them loose.

"Go ahead and give the trapezes a try. Hopefully, you guys are good enough to replace my last flyers."

Well! Did he get the surprise of his life! These guys saw the high wire and the trapeze and thought they had died and gone to heaven.

They played follow the leader with a little free expression thrown in. The leader was up the ladder to the high wire in an instant, not walking across the wire but jumping on it, so it swayed when the other guys followed him. Did that bother these guys? Not a chance!

They started skipping with it, like doing Double Dutch except it was only one wire. The circus guy was so entranced by their activities that he failed to notice the odd hover in the play. (Humans rarely hover in the open air because this thing called gravity gets in the way... if you choose to believe in it!)

And the trapeze! They would get it going so fast that when they swung off it to catch the other swing, you had to have high-speed film to see them. They were flying so fast! The craziest part was that they were not even spacing between jumpers. They were doing it as fast as they could get on the swing... and no one was smacking into another!

The owner missed all these little anomalies. All he saw was the money he was going to make when people came to see his new and improved circus!

Once the gang had finished having their fun on the acrobatic equipment, they were ready for a break. The owner was excited to take them for a tour around the rest of the circus. When they saw the lions and tigers, they giggled and ran right up to their cages! At first, the animals acted so-o tough. They roared, and they scratched on their cage bars, but soon conceded when the boys did not run for their lives. Once they realized the jig was up, they looked down at them and laughed, then plopped themselves down and went to sleep.

Because these boys had been taught to have good manners, they decided to let sleeping lions sleep. However, later on, they came back and took turns going for rides on the lions and tigers. Everybody had fun! The lions, especially, appreciated being brought out of their ruts, so they began licking the boys' faces. Yuk!

They were having so much fun, especially once the news got out about the exciting new performers at the circus, that they almost forgot why they were in this town to start with.

Papi had stayed clear of these antics on purpose, so had Songbird. They felt they needed to stay present in case someone needed their help. When Papi returned from working with Lindsay, she filled Songbird in.

"They are heading over to the war zone tomorrow to begin collecting the children. We need to be ready to jump in when they need us."

"What about the other guys from the third group? They look a little distracted. They might be resentful if they have to give up their fun, and what about the circus owner? He is not going to be happy his circus gets shut down without notice?" Songbird questioned.

"Do you remember when Rachel said there would be a test to determine one's mettle? This could be it. The success of this project, in part, depends on the third group being involved. We will have to let them make their own decisions; however, the owner and the circus will be easier to handle when the time comes," Papi replied.

---

The next morning arrived in an instant. Although the men were nervous about their part in this project, they knew many people were counting on them, so they were eager to get started.

The task this morning was one of reconnaissance. Their job was to inspect any of the buildings in the neighborhood in search of children hiding out. Far from any active fighting, they felt safe enough, but one needed to be on their toes, even with their high level of training.

Keeping together in a group, they would enter buildings after ensuring it was safe. As an added measure, only at a maximum of two at a time entered each search site. The others would wait outside, watching the area. Then they entered one at a time as safety allowed, if they were needed. Each person was completely reliant only on their physical and intuitive senses. There were no devices available to help them out.

The first person in would yell and listen to see if they heard any kind of human-type noise. They would have to inspect each floor of the building, ensuring the building was empty.

It was a sad and difficult task for all of them as they looked inside what used to be beautiful buildings that were now little more than piles of rubble, if even that. The fighting had caused some buildings to be decimated to the point they could not even go inside. They were just piles of brick.

"What makes me especially sad is the fact that people had built these beautiful buildings. Now they lay in ruins, likely destroyed by these same men! A complete waste of resources and beauty for no valid reason." Raven said to no one in particular.

" We have our work cut out for us, but we knew that even before we were born. We knew our lives would be full of challenges trying to help Homo Sapiens to understand. It sure is hard to get them to understand that this kind of waste was in opposition to the desires of the Universal Consciousness and to their own spiritual evolution," Condor replied back.

Throughout the morning, they searched buildings with no contact with any children. In one way, they felt pleased, since maybe they had found their way home and were with their parents. One could only hope!

They returned to their shelter for a short rest and some food, then returned to the streets to continue the search. No luck.

When they returned that evening, tired and sad, they debriefed themselves. It was a long and quiet evening that seemed to last forever.

"Somehow I was under the illusion that we would just waltz in and have a bus load of children on their way to their new homes in only a matter of hours. This is really frustrating. There are so many buildings to investigate. What was it, sixteen buildings we did today and never came across even any evidence of children having been there. I sure hope tomorrow goes better," Raven said as he flopped into a chair.

The next morning, before they headed out, Lindsay's phone rang. It was the man. He wanted to meet with them to discuss what to do with the children once they had collected some.

The meeting place was in a park on the other side of the town. There were no restaurants open, so the park was the easiest place for the man to direct them to. He did not want to stay around for long, because he did not want to be seen with them in case they got caught, so he rushed them over to an old barn that sat near a burned-out house on the edge of town.

He slipped into the barn and motioned them to follow him. After their last episode of going into buildings with him, they were quite hesitant, so only Condor and Phoenix went in at first, but then they realized this time, he went in first, so it should be okay.

Inside the barn, the man took a rake and started dragging it across the floor, looking for a trapdoor. After a few minutes, the rake caught on something, the ring handle of a trap door!

Finding it, he pulled it open, then peered in. He turned to the men and said, "I was told there was a bomb shelter in this barn! It is empty, so this will work as a holding place for the short term. Let me know when you have your first lot, and I will arrange for blankets, water, and food. I don't want to spoil the cargo!"

With that, he disappeared.

This day was discouraging as well. They found no children, even though they had searched over a dozen buildings.

"This is ridiculous!" grumbled Goose. "Why are we doing this the hard way? Let's get Papi here. She has a good nose for finding lost children!"

"I can do it too!" shouted Hummingbird. And before anyone could say anything, he transformed himself into his bird form and was gone.

"We were not supposed to do that!" Goose said. "We need to stay in our human form in case the man shows up! Now we will have to explain why we are missing one person if Hummingbird does not get back before then!

---

With his bird ears on, Hummingbird could now focus on what he was looking for, much more easily than with his human ears. Soon, he could hear the whimpering of what he thought were small children, so he followed the sound. It was close to their resting place, so it only took a couple of minutes.

When he determined which building the noise was coming from, he found an opening, and rushed right... into a trap!

In seconds, Hummingbird was lying on the floor, unable to fly. Someone had set a trap by installing a recording of children crying behind a high-frequency invisible door intended to knock out a grown man. You can imagine what it would do to a little Hummingbird!

Condor had connected with Hummingbird with his mind as he had flown out the door, so as soon as he felt Hummingbird in trouble, he got the guys heading for him. When they reached the building, they stopped outside to look over the situation.

Hummingbird's entry into the building had not done enough damage to the electronic door, so it was still intact. Goose looked around and found a huge chunk of roofing sheet metal laying nearby. He picked it up and threw it through the door, missing Hummingbird. The door exploded and shut down.

They raced in to find their friend. He was still in his bird form, laying hurt.

"Hummingbird, can you hear me?" Goose said as he leaned over his injured friend. "You must turn yourself back into human so we can help you."

But Hummingbird just lay there. Condor reached into his mind to talk to him. "Hummingbird, you must turn yourself back into human, so we can help you.... Please, my friend."

Hummingbird looked at Condor, then telepathed back to him. "I do not deserve your help; I was so selfish, running off like that. You must go on without me!"

"That is not the way of a Wind Surfer, Hummingbird!" Condor replied. "Now quit feeling sorry for yourself and let's help you get whole again. We need you!"

Soon, Hummingbird reverted to his human form. Although it did not appear that he had any broken bones, it was apparent that he had sustained some injuries that would make it difficult for him to move.

Goose looked at him and said, "Hummingbird, you are an authentic person, you can heal yourself."

He stayed quiet for a minute, then he continued, "Hummingbird, see yourself as a whole and complete healthy human being. Visualize yourself as the perfect being you are."

It did not take long until they could see Hummingbird's energy change from the injured victim to the whole and perfect person they all knew and loved. Within minutes, they were all on their way, walking back to their hideout.

Before Hummingbird could say anything, Lindsay looked at him and said, "Do you remember what Rachel said about the importance of being selfless? I guess today was lesson day for you." Lindsay then slapped him on his back, and they all ran back, hoping that Papi was waiting for them.

They were all feeling rather tired from this latest turn of events, so they decided they should just sit and rest for a bit. While they were doing this, Goose contacted Papi to speak with her.

He then turned back to the gang and said, "Papi won't get here until tomorrow. She says the circus is on, so she is going to do her part there because it is not safe for her to be rooting around in buildings like Hummingbird did this late in the day, so she will be here first thing in the morning."

"That girl doesn't miss a beat, does she? Her intuition had already told her about Hummingbird!" Lindsay laughed.

Just then, Lindsay's phone rang. It was the man wanting to know why they had not caught any children. Standing in the barn, looking down through the access hole, he was not a happy camper again!

Lindsay looked shaken. He knew upsetting this man would not bode well for them. They needed to step up their game!

---

The next morning when Goose woke up, Papi was sitting on his nose, fortunately in her butterfly form. She wiggled her wings at him as she saw his eyes open. He smiled and whispered good morning to her.

She then flew to the floor and returned to her human form.

As they all ate their breakfast, Goose filled Papi in on what had occurred so far. They were feeling a little panicky at the moment, so they wanted her to help them. What did Papi think she could do to pick up the pace of the search? This was what they all wanted to know.

Papi just smiled her little butterfly smile, but said nothing until breakfast was complete. She then waved her arms in the air... and thirty more butterflies appeared in the room!

"While we have been playing at the circus, I have been training the others to listen and hear for the children chatting and crying. I also taught them how to use their night vision during the day to see any kinds of electronic traps that might get them into trouble. We do not want to experience what Hummingbird went through!"

That said, the butterflies headed off in an enormous flock to search for children in need of their rescuing. Papi had only taught them how to telepath with her, so she told them to check in with her every few minutes to let them know they were okay. They could be done without difficulty because she had assigned them each a unique color to send to her for that purpose.

When they found any children, they also had a code. Once they had found them, they were to send a message to Papi so she could determine their location, and then she would send the message to Goose.

---

With over thirty Butterflies on the lookout for the children, they were able to spread out wide over the town, so it did not take long for them to find some of the children they were looking for.

They found six groups of children right away hiding inside ruined buildings. The children did not see the butterflies fly in, so they were completely unaware they had been found. Once the men got the message, this made it easier for the men to find them.

The men stayed together as they moved from one site to the next. This was not a straightforward task for them. The children were terrified of adults, so they resisted being removed from their hiding places, however; they were all pretty hungry, so finally, with the help of a little Golden Butterfly, they agreed to go with the men.

As they went from one hiding place to another, they found a good place to hide them together, so Condor and Hummingbird agreed to stay with them while the others finished the collections.

As they had moved the children into the bomb shelter in the barn, Goose conjured up some superb food for them. So, as they climbed down the ladder, they set aside their fears... at least, mostly.

---

Several of the little butterflies opted to stay with the children, while the rest returned to the search. With Papi and the men, they returned to the streets to find as many children as they could that day. The men were feeling the pressure from the discussion earlier in the day with the man. However, there was another unknown pressure they felt but could not identify as yet.

They found another three groups of children during the afternoon and brought them to the shelter. They were very pleased that this new method was working so well. Amazing what a little teamwork can accomplish!

They hoped to be as successful the next day, but they knew this day had completely done them in, so they stayed with the children for the night and would start again bright and early after a good sleep.

They were immediately glad they stayed. The butterfly show entertained them all evening. They just seemed to have never-ending energy. The children laughed as the butterflies swooped down and flew up, sometimes together, sometimes alone. They even did rollovers and cannonballs! One would think they were at a circus!

Later in the evening, they could hear footsteps above them. They suspected it was the man, but it sounded like there was more than one person. They did not talk at all, so it was hard to determine how many.

No one came down the stairs, so it was hard to determine who it was, but no one felt it necessary to investigate.

Not long after the noise above stopped, everyone started feeling sleepy, then dozed off. The men were feeling it too but realized too late. They were being gassed!

---

The men woke up sometime later, only to find themselves alone. Even the third group had been affected. The gas had returned them to their human forms, so it was still pretty crowded in there!

Once they were awake enough to realize, they knew it had been the man who had been walking around upstairs earlier. He had been preparing to complete his trap. The man had completely fooled them!

As they looked around, they discovered a side door to the shelter they had not noticed before. This must have been how they removed the children. Unfortunately, they had locked the door from the outside. Phoenix immediately climbed the ladder to check the trap door. They had also locked it.

This was definitely a problem! But not insurmountable for these people, since they should be able to just project themselves outside, then open one door. This gas that had caused them to go to sleep, though, had messed with their minds, making it so that they could not focus enough to do anything except sit. Now what?

# Chapter 9

Mike and Tomas had been keeping themselves busy watching the man. They knew Lindsay and the crew were out trying to find and rescue the children, so they had focused on the activities of this man and his other accomplices. This was a full-time occupation on its own!

They had used their special skills a few times to check in more closely during conversations, but they had not used more than their human skills of observation to do their part in the project. They did transition from male to female, just for practical disguise on occasion, though.

This man excelled at his profession. He was a very devious person and kept many of his cards close to his chest. Even his accomplices often were caught off guard when he took a right turn when they expected a left turn. This man was nobody's fool.

One day, for example, he had been doing some prep work for the transport of the children. He had a group of six men who were preparing a cellar in an old barn. The room was an old root cellar where the farmers had stored their food crops for winter use.

Their job was to dig the root cellar out so it would become more like a bomb shelter. It was real grunt work, digging a huge room out by hand, underneath a barn, no less. By the time they had finished it, it was large enough to hold about fifty adults. As soon as they had completed the job, the man appeared with plenty of food and alcohol for the men. He said he wanted to show them some appreciation for their efforts.

As the men were hungry from all the work, they dove right away into their gift. They liked to be appreciated and had certainly earned their keep. After all, they had just completed a momentous task! Within an hour, they were all lying about on the ground, fast asleep.

This accomplished, the man-made a phone call. A bit later, a large truck arrived with several men inside. They loaded the sleeping men into the truck and disappeared. In a flash, these men were no longer on the payroll.

---

The man had staked one other man to stay near the shelter as an observer, so he always knew what was going on. That incited the first meeting with Lindsay, where he protested they had captured no children at all after two days of searching. However, it also incited the resulting success that occurred soon after.

It thrilled him when the observer reported to him that the group had captured and stowed over one hundred children in the shelter. This was what he had been waiting for!

Mike and Tomas watched the man enter the barn a while later, but could not get close enough to observe what he was doing. When he came out, he and the observer left. They noticed nothing unusual about his visit to the barn at that juncture, so they followed him, not knowing that another group of men was waiting in the trees near the barn.

The men had noticed Mike and Tomas standing nearby, so the leader had dispatched some of the men to sneak in behind them. The plan was to capture them once they were sure that the man had completed whatever he had planned and left.

As the men sneaked up on Mike and Tomas, they found themselves waist-deep in a mucky mire filled with plants and roots that wrapped around their legs. As they attempted to extricate themselves, they looked at each other. "How is this possible?" showed all over their faces. After all, this was not swamp country!

The captured men were too busy trying to get themselves out, so they did not think to yell for help. In the meantime, Mike and Tomas continued watching the scene unfold before them. Since the rest of the group of men who had stayed in the trees were now in between them and the escaping man, they stayed so they could find out what they were up to.

It was a good thing they did stay! About fifteen minutes after the man left, one man entered the barn but returned right away. Then they all walked to one end of the barn where the ground dropped away to the floor level of the bomb shelter.

He walked up to the wall of the cellar, removed some boards exposing a door. Once done, he opened the door, then stepped back.

They looked like they were waiting for something as they stood further back from the barn. About thirty minutes later, a truck arrived. The truck driver retrieved a large box from the back of the truck. It was full of gas masks.

Mike and Tomas realized they were here to retrieve the captured children. What better way to move them than to put them all to sleep! No muss! No fuss! And especially- no whiny brats!

All they could do was stand by and watch the precious children being loaded into the truck. Once done, the truck headed off to who knows where while the men who had done the dirty work walked away like they had just finished their shifts at the mill.

They were so self-absorbed; they did not even notice that the men who had attempted to capture Mike and Tomas had not returned.

Merle appeared so she could read the minds of these men, to see if they knew where the truck was going. There was nothing of use wandering inside the minds of these men. At that point, Merle made the swamp disappear, leaving the men sitting on a rocky patch. This event had scared them so much, they just ran away like rabbits into the bush, likely to find a church where they could confess their sins!

---

Amid all the activity going on, no one had noticed a little Golden Butterfly had nestled in the pocket of one little boy's jacket.

# Chapter 10

Mike and Tomas waited for quite a while before they ventured near the cellar. They wanted to make sure that there were none of the man's people lurking about or that any might come back. Once they felt it was safe, they picked up two of the discarded gas masks, then opened the side door and ventured into the cellar.

They did not even have time to get inside the cellar because as soon as they opened the door, everybody inside the room came staggering out. It was quite a procession; thirty of the third class, all the Wind Surfers, and, of course, Lindsay.

It took a few minutes for each of them to clear their lungs and their heads, but; they felt awake again and ready to discuss this situation. It took them a few minutes more to realize they were missing one very important person!

Papi woke up from a very long nap. That gas had done her right in, knocking her out cold. She felt very cozy in her pocket nest, so she lay there until she could get her wits about her. The little butterfly then climbed out so she could have a look at the situation.

All the children were still unconscious, but where were they? She hopped up high into the box they were in to look around. She looked down at the boy whose pocket she had slipped into. It was a good thing she got into her safe place when she did. It would have been very uncomfortable if the gas had caused her to return to her human form! Now that would have been uncomfortable!

Anyway, she had managed to remain in butterfly and now she could figure out what was going on. She could feel that whatever they were in was moving, so she concluded they must be in the back of a big truck. Flying around a bit, Papi tried to see if she could find a place to look outside, but they had sealed the box. It became apparent, the best thing to do was to sit and wait. Sometime in the future, she would find out their destination.

Once she was feeling herself again, she tried to connect with Goose.

---

As the men discussed the situation, they were also trying to figure out what their next step should be. At one point, Goose explored the area, then went back into the cellar.

On his return, he looked at the others and said, "Papi is not here. I wonder if she managed to hide with the children so she could go with them."

Mike then replied, "That does sound like something she would do. Looks like she is going to be the hero in our adventure here. Goose, maybe you should try to reach out to her."

Goose then went over to a beautiful cedar tree, then went into meditation. It did not take long for him to realize that Papi was trying to reach him. Once they connected, the conversation was just like they were standing together under the cedar tree.

"I am ok," said Papi. "Just as I felt the gas blowing into the cellar, I jumped into a little boy's pocket, hoping that being in there would protect me. It had not even occurred to me that by doing this, I would end up going with the children. By and by, I fell asleep, then I woke up where I am now."

"Well, I am glad you are okay, my friend. It is fortunate that you did what you did because now you can be our tracking device. We are still at the barn, everybody is ok. All the third group are here, but they transformed back into human form when the man's accomplices released the gas," said Goose.

"Can you transport yourself outside the truck, so you can get an idea of where you are and where the truck is heading?"

"Let me get back to you when I have more information. I am still feeling a little off. I need to focus so I can see if I can get outside. Chat with you soon!" she said.

Goose reported his conversation to the others, then suggested they comb the area to see if they left any clues behind. After that, they could walk back into town to get some food. They would need all their strength and wits about them to catch up to Papi.

Nothing resulted from the search, so they walked the short distance back into town. They headed for the restaurant the man had fed them at earlier in the week. Phoenix thought it might be worthwhile trying to have a chat with the owner again to see what he knew about the man.

Once they had eaten, Phoenix sauntered up to the man to pay the bill. Then, as they completed the payment, he asked if the owner might have any idea where the man might have gone.

The owner suggested they might consider checking out some of the towns near the coast. There was one town in particular that had a good-sized port where larger boats could tie up. With the war raging in the interior, the officials were not so likely to be interested in smaller private craft so they could load up and ship out unnoticed.

When Phoenix reported the information to the group, Mike agreed with the information, then said, "This whole thing came together so fast that Tomas and I did not even have time to look at the lay of the land. We knew there were towns along the coast but had not stopped to peruse the situation to determine what was available to him."

Tomas then said, "I think we should head out that way. It seems to make sense that he would go to water, as our information we received before seemed to show that he planned to hold the children on an island."

All agreed that made sense, but what made little sense right now was to have an entourage of about 40 people, so Mike suggested that the third group head back to the circus for now, but to be ready to jump in again when needed.

---

It seemed strange to be sitting in such a small group again when they got together the next morning. Mike had hired a bus to take them to the city that the restaurant owner had suggested. With the exception of Lindsay, they could have teleported themselves but after a brief discussion on the subject, they decided it would be of more value to take the time it would take to go by bus. That way, they could have a bit of a look at the countryside.

Mike thought that, even though they may not need to come back inland, it would still be useful to get a look at the countryside, as it might reveal clues about the people that might help in fulfilling the needs of this project.

That said, they arrived in the port town about four hours later. Everyone except Mike went to find a roost for themselves for whatever time they needed to be in this town, while Mike went to report to the local police.

Merle pointed out a bit of a problem with Mike's desire as they headed off on their own. Mike had forgotten that they were in a foreign country where they rarely spoke English.

"Hmmm. That is a bit of a problem, my dear. Do you have any suggestions?"

"Let's find somewhere out of the way where we can sit for a bit. We need some privacy. I would like to try something with you," Merle replied.

They walked for a while until they found a small park up on a knoll. Mike looked around to see if there were any other visitors, but found none. He then found a nice bench to sit on that overlooked the city. It was a beautiful view and a great place to chat.

"What I would like to try something we have never tried before. I think that after all the amazing things we have learned, we might learn one more.

The challenge we have here is that you have the reputation, so they know you all over the world. However, I am the one who can speak any language I need.

What I would like to try here is to see if I can speak out loud when I am on the inside. It might sound kind of funny because my voice is higher in pitch but then, they don't know what your voice sounds like."

Mike laughed and said, "This sounds like fun. Let's give it a go."

Merle tried and tried, but she could not project her voice outside when she was not out there. She kept trying for over an hour. After at least an hour, Mike stopped her.

"I have another suggestion that we might try," he said, "but first, let's take a few minutes to rest and connect with Source. This is pretty heavy-duty stuff!"

After a bit of a rest, Mike said to her, "Okay, let's take a fresh approach. I have seen when people are trying to speak a foreign language, they tend to speak quite slowly, and they have to stop often to think about how to say what they want.

My suggestion is for me to tell you in English what I want to say, then you tell me how to say it, and then I will attempt to say it to the person we are talking with. Does that sound workable, Merle?"

"Let's give it a try!" she said, then went quiet so she could listen to Mike's thoughts.

Mike started by introducing himself to the desk officer. Merle then translated his introduction. With a lot of coaching, Mike got it, sort of.

They continued practicing various bits of conversation for quite a long time. It did seem to be a way to make this work. Then Merle realized she would also have to translate what the other person speaking said to Mike, then let him give an answer to Merle, so she could translate it.

Merle was going to be one tired girl after this activity! Merle then suggested that they should wait until the next day to see the police. What they might do today... is go shopping!

"You aren't going to buy me a new outfit, are you?" Mike laughed and got his usual kick. "So what you want to do is practice this technique first on some folks that we don't have to impress, right?"

"Let's send a message to the others for now and tell them we will be a few hours, so they don't worry about us."

When they arrived at the downtown area of the city, Mike suggested they go for a meal first. He was feeling a little hungry, so this would accomplish two tasks at one time.

When they sat down in a little restaurant, the server came over and said hello and asked if he wanted a menu. Merle told Mike what to say. At first, he hesitated, but then he repeated what she had said.

The server smiled, then brought Mike a menu, coffee, and water-no ice. Mike smiled at her, then chuckled to himself. Merle kicked him again.

After a few minutes, the server came back and just stood by the table. Mike looked up at her, smiled, and told her correctly what Merle had told him. Such cooperation!

After lunch, they perused a lady's clothing store. Mike had a bit of an issue with that because he could not explain why he wanted to look at women's clothing that would fit a woman about his size. Merle laughed and laughed, reminiscing of days of old!

Just to get back at her, as they walked down the street, he walked into a hardware store and started checking out power tools. This girl was not to be fazed, though. She got right in there and made Mike look like he was a native, well, a very slow speaking native... but still!

They decided since it was getting late in the afternoon after all this practicing that they should find Lindsay and the gang so they can relax and settle in for the night. Mike sat down so he could focus his mind, then reached out to Goose to get directions to their location.

It was quite a way to walk to where the gang was holed up, so Mike and Merle swapped just to let her have a better look at the outside world... and to breathe her own air for once. It had been quite a long time that she had been inside.

Merle had not been walking for very long when she stopped and stared. Coming right at her, down the street was a large truck similar to the one that Papi had described, and Mike had seen at the barn.

There was a bus bench right near where they were walking, so she sat down and focused her mind so she could call Papi.

When Papi replied, Merle asked, "Are any of the children awake yet? If they are, please get them to make loud noises. We are right near a truck, like Mike saw at the barn. It might be the one you are in!"

Sure enough, almost immediately, they could hear childlike noises filtering out of the truck. They now knew they were in the right town. It was very hard for a big truck like this one to move at any kind of speed because of the narrow streets, so it was easy for Merle to follow it.

One of the great things about being Homo integratis is that one is always of two minds, literally! Merle continued following the truck while Mike contacted Goose to update him. It might be a good thing for the gang to start heading over this way.

Merle planned to follow this truck to its destination. The trick would for her be not to be seen! She had two things going for her that made this job easier; first, no one over here knew her, and second, she was a master of disguise. It was quite a long walk, so she would nip out of sight every once in a while, reappearing behind the truck wearing a different outfit.

It was a good thing they had stopped for lunch because this turned out to be quite the walk. This was quite a large city, but it was old, at least in this part, so the drive was slow through the narrow streets, allowing her to keep constant sight of the truck.

After a while, it occurred to Mike to ask Merle why the truck was taking this route if this was a big city. Didn't it make sense that if it were going to the port, it would just take the highway to it?

Merle smiled, giving Mike a big hug. "That is a good point, Mike! You are so smart! I am going to check into the mind of the driver and see what I can come up with. They are driving so slow we won't lose them if I stop for a few minutes."

Merle leaned up against a light post, trying to make it look like she was waiting for someone, then closed her eyes. She projected her mind to the mind of the truck driver to see if she could connect. Since he felt no need to protect himself, she then asked him where he was going. The driver never even knew the conversation had occurred, but now Merle knew the truck's destiny.

Before she opened her eyes, she contacted both Papi and Goose to let them know the ship they had contracted for the trip was not in town yet. It had been delayed, so they were taking the children to a warehouse to store them until the ship could dock and be readied.

Papi then told Merle that when they arrived there, she needed to return to human form for a while, as she felt exhausted. (It takes a lot of energy to stay in Butterfly when your natural form is human!)

They needed to have someone watching the children, so Merle contacted Tomas.

When the truck arrived at the warehouse, the first thing that happened as they opened the back door of the truck, (unbeknownst to the bad guys!) the two butterflies exchanged places.

The children were all awake, so the men just lifted them down onto the ground and pointed to the warehouse. They were all tired from the long uncomfortable drive and starving, so they were not up to giving an argument. They just staggered into the building and flopped where they could.

With no consideration for the children, the men closed up the truck, locked the door on the storage facility, and drove away! No food, no water, nothing to care for the children!

Merle did not get angry very often, but today was her day! How can people be so uncaring?

Mike suggested she stay away from the building for a bit just to make sure no one was going to show up, so she sat there fuming, desperately wanting to go in and help Tarita with the children.

About fifteen minutes later, Lindsay and the gang came walking along. Merle told them about the situation. Lindsay offered to stand guard since he could not teleport himself, while the others headed into the building. If anything needed their attention on the outside, Lindsay was to whistle like a certain bird. (Songbird had taught him that!)

Inside the building, Tarita was busy fluttering about, trying to calm the children. This was no easy task, as there were over one hundred tired and hungry people in this tiny space!

No food trucks to call in on this project, so Goose conjured up a banquet of food for the children, with lots of water and juice to drink. He had to repeat it several times since the children were so hungry.

They seemed to settle down after they had fed themselves, so creature comfort was next on the list. (Merle must have been a great mom in another lifetime!) She asked Phoenix and Condor to work together to manifest everything the little ones would need, so they could clean themselves up. Showers with warm water, soap, towels, and even changes of clothes were waiting for them at the side of the room in an instant.

The last thing Merle concluded the children would need would be some bedding. Poof! Now the place was starting to look like it was a little civilized!

Almost as soon as the children had cleaned up, they climbed into a bed and dozed off. This had been a terrible ordeal for them... and it was far from over.

# Chapter 11

The man was fuming that the boat was late arriving. He knew there was not much he could do about it. His original plan had not included storing the children in a warehouse for the duration of the hold-up. He accepted they were precious cargo (more cargo than precious!) so, therefore, he would need to make some provisions for them.

He did not want to go to the warehouse himself, and after their recent treatment, the children would fear the men, so that would not work either. What to do?

Then he realized that several of the men lived in this town, and they were married. What a convenient solution! He contacted them right away, asking them to organize their wives to look after the children. They would need to purchase some food and drinks for them, but nothing more. He was not giving up any more of his money than necessary.

The man told the men he was not willing to pay the women for their time. He would credit it as goodwill for them. Being the kind of men they were, there was little grumbling.

The women were not even going to be driven to the stores to purchase the supplies or to haul the supplies to the warehouse. This did not make them any happier.

Merle had decided to check in on this man, so she was aware of what he was planning to do. For the second time in so many days, she was not happy! She recalled that Rachel, though, had mentioned there would be opportunities to see how well entrenched in the energy of love there would be. Selfish or selfless!

Merle calmed herself down and spent a little time reconnecting with Source. Once she had herself back together, she got busy and created a plan to usher the women into the warehouse. Inside, they could do their work and be off to home... maybe with a little surprise for their husbands!

A bit later, Papi returned to the scene after having a good sleep, so she replaced Tarita. Now she could help Merle out with the wives. As she joined Merle, Tarita could see she was in deep thought. It looked like she was trying to figure out a hard puzzle.

"What are you thinking about, my friend? Maybe I can help."

"I am trying to figure out how to connect with the women who are coming here today. They will bring food for the children. I want to prepare them before they arrive, so it does not mess up what we have already done. The problem is that I do not know how to connect my mind to a person I don't know. I need a target," Merle replied.

They sat together and meditated on the problem for a few minutes. Tarita then said, "What if I fly over the area and look for a grocery store nearby, then look for a group of women shopping together?"

"Great idea, Tarita! Let's see if you can find them before they get to shopping. This way, they will still be disorganized as a group. If you can, try to pick out one that seems to be the leader so we can focus on her."

"Yes, then I could land on her and maybe try to make her laugh so I can connect with her. Then you can get into her mind more easily."

And on that note, Tarita fluttered off in search of a group of women who might be their target. As she flew off, Tarita focused her mind on Merle so they would be in communication during this procedure.

Because of the military situation inland, there was a lot of tension in the town. This offered a much easier opportunity for Tarita as few people were out walking on the street, even if it was the middle of the day. Before long, Tarita spied a group of six women walking toward her. They looked like women who had put up with the kind of men they were married to; the kind that abandoned children with no food or water!

Tarita moved in to listen to their conversation. She could not understand their words, but she could understand the intonations. These women were not happy; because they were not getting paid for their effort. They also did not want to meddle in their husbands' nefarious affairs.

At first, Tarita stayed out of sight, trying to determine if one woman seemed likely to be leading the group. Once she figured out which one the leader was, she fluttered close to her without landing.

It surprised the woman that a beautiful butterfly was flying near her. It surprised her even more, when it landed on her shoulder, content to ride along. She had never befriended a butterfly before, and now, even though she was feeling furious, she let her guard down to enjoy the company of her new friend.

Once Tarita had gotten the woman's attention, Merle seized the opportunity to link with the woman's mind. She then made suggestions to her regarding the food and other necessities to buy.

The next step was to create suggestions in her mind to convey to the other women. It was important, they do not notice the condition of the children. They were in much better condition than they should have been, considering the poor treatment they had received from their host so far.

Tarita stayed with the women throughout their journey to the warehouse, keeping Merle updated along the way. When the women were nearby, Lindsay went for a walk while the others made themselves invisible. At the last moment, Goose made all the bedding and bathroom area disappear.

When they arrived, the lead woman took a key out of her pocket and let the others in. It appalled them to see the condition of the children. She said to the other women that this was unacceptable, for any reason. Children should never be treated so poorly!

They knew, however, that there was little time for them to help the children. Not speaking their dialect, they placed the food on the floor, then pointed at it, telling the children to eat it.

As the women were about to leave, Guardian Angel Rachel appeared before them. They shook in their boots when they saw her. They were all religious women, but they had experienced nothing like this before.

Rachel looked down at them, smiling, then said, *"I am Rachel. I serve the Universal God that created this earth and all that exists. I invite you to join me in this moment of knowing yourself through the eyes of God."*

She paused for a moment, allowing the women to get past their emotions and resistance.

*"You have done great service by assisting these children. We know you feel helpless in your situation and in your life, but please accept that it is your choice to continue living as you do. You are free to be who you choose to be. You are also free to choose who you associate with. You can choose to live your life on purpose as servants of the Cosmic, or you can choose to continue to be servants of your men. It is up to you."*

Rachel stopped again for a moment, letting the women absorb her words.

*"If you choose to continue to be the servants of your men, you may return to your homes, and all will continue as is. If you choose to give your life to the Universal God who created all, you will return home as servants of God. You will know the choice you have each made when you*

*return to your homes. Remember, you can only truly serve the God of*
*your heart, by knowing and being who you are."*

As Rachel finished, she smiled, then faded away. After a while,
the women began walking back to their homes.

It would be a lesson for the men to never mess with empowered
women.

---

The next day, the man was outraged. These men, who he had
hired to do his dirty work, decided they would stay home with their
wives for the day. Their women had inspired them to become better
people, so they thought they should spend some time with them.

"What is this world coming to?" he grumbled.

In the meantime, back at the warehouse, everyone was busy
helping the children. There were a lot of children that needed their
help. The older children realized nine adults could not do the job
well enough, so they pitched in by helping wherever they were
needed and by playing with the younger children.

After they had finished their morning cleanup and breakfast, she
had them all sit on their beds. She wanted to have a discussion with
them to help them understand what was going on and what was
going to happen to them.

Merle began her chat by saying, "We are here to help you, as you
can see. However, things will not be easy, and they will not make
sense for now. I need you to trust us, that everything will turn out
okay if you will do as we ask.

It is our intention, once this ordeal is over, to take you home with
us to our home. You will live with us for as long as you choose. We
will help you move past the hurts you feel today, and the frustrations
you will feel in the near future.

Soon, the men will come to move you again. This time they will
take you to a ship that is supposed to carry you to some far-off land.
We will be watching everything that happens, even if you do not

see us. You must be good little actors and pretend that these people scare you, then do what he asks. He cannot find out we have been helping you. It could cause problems for us to rescue you when the time comes."

Merle let what she said soak in, then one brave little boy said to her, "What can you do to prove to us we can trust you, and that you will come back for us?"

Before Merle could even answer the question, the room was filled with butterflies.

She smiled at the boy, then asked the crowd, "Does this answer your concerns?"

---

Two days later, the truck pulled up outside the warehouse. They were ready for the next step in their adventure. They were ready for the truck to arrive as well. Lindsay had kept a constant vigil outside the warehouse, acting as eyes for Merle. Merle checked in as needed with the man to determine how his plans were progressing.

She had learned the day before that the ship had docked and they were outfitting it for the children's voyage to who knows where. They did not know what the conditions were going to be like on the ship. There was genuine concern the children would not get much food during the voyage. To ensure their health, they made sure they all got fed well during their stay in the warehouse. Besides reassuring and feeding them, there was little more they could do.

The children seemed to be ready to move forward. They were feeling more confident than when they had arrived. Who could want for anything more when they have an ensemble of beautiful butterflies to escort them? These children needed nothing else.

By the time the truck arrived, they had removed all the bedding and cleaned up the facilities.... And the adults had disappeared (literally!). The children had learned how to pretend to act scared and distraught so the men would not notice anything odd. However, when the men walked through the door, Merle spoke to their higher selves and asked them to not notice that the children were any different from earlier.

The men who came in were the same ones who had delivered them, but they were different. They were kind to the children, treating them like humans instead of cargo. None of them noticed the children were all clean and wearing new clothes, though. Maybe they just thought their wives had done an amazing job of providing for them!

# Chapter 12

The ship was no luxury liner, but it was pretty big. It had to be to house one hundred children for whatever time it was going to take to get to their destination. The man was on board, which was something he had never done before. He did not like to be associated with his cargo!

After the event on the last ship he used, though, he was not willing to take chances. This cargo was going to make it to its rightful place!

The men who had manned the truck were not on board. There were enough crew members to babysit for the brief journey, so he had sent them packing. He was glad to get rid of them, anyway. They sure were acting weird, and he wanted none of that!

It pleased him that the children had all cooperated during the transport onto the ship. He had expected a lot of resistance, but they just filed onto the boat and went where they were directed. Maybe they were feeling a little more settled after the men's wives had gone out of their way to feed them.

He chuckled to himself, then decided that if they were that well-fed, he could save himself a little more cash by not feeding them during the voyage. After all, fasting is good for you, someone had told him once.

A crew member left some bottles of water inside the door of the room where the children were, but other than that, no one bothered them for the entire trip. Even though they were getting a little hungry, they felt excited about the future. Who wouldn't be with thirty-one butterflies to entertain you and lead you forward!

---

Two days later, they arrived at their destination. The children could not see outside, but they knew they had reached a port because they heard and felt the boat hit the dock. In fact, it hit the dock a little hard and damaged the wharf. Do you think the man was a little ticked, maybe?

It took a while to get the ship docked to the damaged wharf, but with a great deal of effort, they got it done. Now they could get their precious cargo off this boat and get on with making some real cash.

As soon as the children were off, the man handed the captain some cash (less an amount to cover ruining his dock!) and told him to get lost. Happily, the captain was in agreement!

The island did not appear to be very big, but the man knew that it would serve his purpose. He led the children up a hill. At the top, they could see a big barn. As they moved toward it, they guessed that this was going to be their new home, at least for a short while.

Once they were inside the barn, a group of very surly-looking men and women came in to survey the situation. Their job was to count the children and assess their needs for clothing. They needed to make the children look as presentable as possible for the prospective buyers. They also brought food and water, at least enough to keep them from starving.

All the butterflies had hidden in jacket pockets of the children, so no one that worked for the man saw them as they came onto the island. After the adults left the barn, they started peering out of the pockets, trying to see if the coast was clear.

As soon as Papi regained her freedom, she flew up to a rafter. She then quieted herself down so she could contact Merle and Tarita. It didn't take long until they were having a three-way telepathic conversation.

They decided they would both show up on the island, but for much different purposes. Tarita was going to work with the children to prepare them for when they became residents of the Matrix. Merle, in the meantime, was going to spy on the man and his people to try to get a handle on what their plans were.

Merle and Tarita would arrive to join Papi around the same time. However, they would get there in their own particular way. Tarita transformed herself into a Golden Butterfly. She then imagined herself sitting beside Papi, and voila, there she was!

Merle used the more conventional method of teleportation since she did not have any butterfly genes. She could only be a butterfly in dreamland... so far.

Tarita and Papi got busy with the other butterflies looking after the needs of the children. The man and his people visited once in a while. They were not interested in being babysitters, so steered clear of the barn otherwise.

Merle did not land inside the barn. She wanted to just look around the island so she could be familiar with anything that might help them with rescuing the children. After a pleasant stroll around the island, she went invisible so she could enter the house where the others were living. It was time to find out if anything was happening.

As she entered the room where the man was sitting at a table, she heard him say, "I have notified all the buyers that we have plenty of excellent stock. When I hear from any of them, we can get the children prepared so we can show them off. We should be able to fetch a good dollar for every one of them." He loved to brag!

Merle did her best to count the people who had come to help the man. She felt it was important to know this so she could keep track of them. She also planned to watch the dock in case anybody new showed up.

A few days later, she was back in the house, hoping to hear something new. She had been tracking him telepathically, but having the opportunity to look at his face gave her much more information. The return phone calls had left him feeling elated. All four of his clients had responded and asked for instructions. The first client was due in about three days, planning to take about twenty of the children.

Merle relayed the information to Tarita, Papi, and Goose.

During the night of the second day, Merle heard a noise coming from around the dock. She thought it odd because none of the clients were due to show up for at least another day. Like the professional spy she is, she moved to a place where she could see the dock. There was a boat tying up. It dawned on her as she watched that they had come early to steal the children so they would not have to pay for them.

She then entered the barn and called Tarita and Papi to alert them of the pending intrusion. Not a moment later, the barn door opened and several men, all dressed in black, entered the room. They did not even bother to look at the children to decide which ones they wanted; they just took the first ones they could grab.

The ladies had agreed that this was a good thing to happen so, they told the children what was about to occur. They told them to go with the people and to cooperate with them.

The men were surprised at how easy their job was. The children grabbed what little they owned, lined up, and tiptoed down to the dock. Within an hour, twenty-four children were on their way to their new home (plus one butterfly!)

Once the boat had left the dock, Merle contacted Goose to apprise him of the situation. It thrilled Goose that they could now get busy, and that the first load of children was free for the picking.

The boat dashed out to open water. The leader of this group figured they would be safer once they were an insignificant speck in a vast body of water. They stowed the children in a room at the bottom of the ship. There was not much room for them to sit or get settled in, so they were feeling very anxious. However, they remained hopeful, especially when Papi reappeared!

Goose waited for Papi to give him the signal. It was late at night, so she watched the crew, hoping that most of them would retire to their beds. This would make it much easier for Goose and the others.

Then the signal! All six of the Wind Surfers projected themselves to the boat. Just for fun, they had dressed up like pirates. How do you think the captain of the boat felt when he turned around in his room on the bridge to find Long John Silver standing in his presence?

Because they all thought they were safely out on the high seas, they were not prepared for visitors. However, there was still one challenge once the crew was subdued- how to get the captain to change his course. No problem!

Merle appeared right after the boys, landing in the bridge right beside Goose, or Long John Silver, in this case. They had not notified her of the required costume for the occasion. However, as she landed, she saw Goose in his pirate outfit, so she transformed herself into a fair damsel!

The captain was still trying to get his head around having a pirate on his bridge when Merle arrived in her very sexy outfit. He just stared at her as she stood in her beautiful gown with her face hiding behind a hand fan.

Before he had a chance to regain his composure, Merle locked into his mind, applied the correct amount of golden energy, and there we are! The boat was now off to the port city near the Matrix.

Merle checked to see what time it was at the Matrix. After all, she did not want to wake up Beth from much-needed sleep, especially since it would take several days to arrive at the port.

The other members had infiltrated the minds of all the crew members. They had decided beforehand that they would recondition the minds of the crew so that they believed they were on a school junket and that the children were special guests of the Royal Family, therefore; they needed to be treated very well indeed!

When the crew members woke up in the morning, they all carried on with their duties, preparing food for the children and helping them to clean themselves up. They had other duties to perform as well, so they left the children to entertain themselves otherwise. They told the children later that they appreciated how mature they were and that everyone got along so well.

Merle decided she needed to get back to the island so she could get everyone ready for the aftermath. First thing in the morning, she contacted Beth so she could alert the authorities of the incoming boat. She then called everyone together to give them an update regarding the twenty-four other children. The Matrix children were all excited when they learned that the next group of children were already on their way to their new home- the Matrix!

No one at the house had heard the boat in the night, so it was a complete surprise to the staff when they arrived to bring breakfast that they noticed the population of their prisoners had decreased! Oops!

It did not take long for the man to break his rule of no personal contact! He had thought that the island was safe to do his business, so he did not post any outside guards. Now he had been duped and was out of twenty-four items. This was going to cost! And somebody was going to pay! But who?

There was no information to be found about who had come in and taken the children during the night. He reached out to his four clients. None of them seemed to know anything!

Well, this would not happen again! He went back to the house, got on the phone, and later that day, another boat arrived. This boat was not docking to pick up children. It had arrived with a dozen very vicious dogs! The dogs' master was the only person who could work with the dogs, so there would be no more interference without the man's knowledge or consent!

The dogs terrified the man's staff with their barking and lunging at everyone. They refused to check in on the children because they did not want to go outside. The man consoled himself that the rest of the children would be in boats going to their new homes within the next couple of days, so it mattered little.

The master of the dogs was skilled at his craft. He positioned the dogs in strategic locations between the barn and the dock. Nobody was going to be wandering around here without his say-so!

Merle headed outside to have a good look at the recent development. She was not afraid of the dogs. In fact, it might turn out they were going to be cowering away from her because of her mastery skills, or she might have to take them all home as pets. She had never wanted to own a kennel, but she needed to have her way with the dogs. Whatever the outcome, all would be okay!

As she wandered about (in the physical), she met the dogs one by one. Their first impulse was to do their guard dog thing. When they stood up to act tough, she just looked at them and helped them to remember when they were little puppies.

Before long, she had befriended all the dogs. Not going to be much good for guard dogs now! However, Merle needed them to pretend for a while, so she called to them again through her mind telephone and asked them to remember being guard dogs, but not to attack anyone. Just make lots of noise when needed. Merle promised each of them that at the end of this job, they would get all the treats and affection they could desire since there were still about seventy-five children in the barn who would love to play with them.

That settled, Merle needed to find out what was going to happen next. There must be a ship due soon. She also wanted to know what the man planned to do about the ship full of children that got away, so she projected herself into the house to have a good listen to all the conversations.

Inside the house, it was utter chaos. The man had been wracking his brain trying to figure out how to get any information regarding the boat that had appeared uninvited during the night. It was not like he could just call up the Coast Guard or the local police and report a burglary. He was on his own on this one. He needed some alone time to think!

The next thing she heard was that the man would receive a boat hired by one of his clients that evening. They planned to pick out the best thirty children and to pay top dollar for them. It thrilled the man about their willingness to compensate him. In fact, he decided they should pay a premium so he could recoup some of his recent losses.

Forgetting about his new visitors, the man ran like a crazy person out the back door of the house, heading to somewhere where he could just sit down and think. He made it up over the hill but soon found himself faced with a more formidable issue- a vicious dog!

He started yelling for the dog master, but he was out of hearing range. The dog kept growling at him, but it made no attempt to charge at him. (After all, he was following Merle's instructions!)

When Merle realized what was happening, she called the dog back. The man thought he was in control because just at that moment; he yelled at the dog and pointed his hand, telling it to remove itself from his presence. (Not in those exact words)

The dog stopped acting like a guard dog, then turned and sauntered away, likely looking to see if he could find a nice bone!

The man sat down under a tree, feeling very shaken by the ordeal. He was not going to figure anything out now. He would have to make decisions by the seat of his pants this day. The missing children would have to wait.

Merle needed him to figure out the plan though, so she sent him some calming golden energy, not too much though, as he still needed to be the man for now.

As he was getting up to move back into the house when he felt a calm come over him, so he sat back down and pondered. The events of the coming evening were coming together with little effort, so they were not much concern, but it was bugging him who had taken those children.

Suddenly, a picture came into his mind that had not occurred to him before! He saw a picture of the boat that he had hired for the last mission... and that captain was piloting it! That fool hacker had been wrong. That boat was not the one that had sunk out in the ocean!

Now he was furious! He was going to get that guy... wherever he was!

Time was moving on, as it always does. It was getting close to nightfall. He needed to prepare for the incoming boat. He called the dog master to move the dogs away so the staff could get to the children. They needed to be at their best when his client arrived.

When the staff entered the barn, the children gave them no mind. They were too busy playing games and having fun. They were all cleaned up already, so the staff just turned around and returned to the house.

When they entered the house, the man questioned them about why they were back so soon. When they told him, he just shook his head. Things were just not adding up!

At last, the boat arrived. The man wanted to make this as quick as possible. As the boat docked, he had the dog master contain the dogs so the client and his crew could walk up to the barn without fear of having some part of their body donated to a dog's nutritional program.

When the client entered the barn, he could not believe his eyes! As soon as he entered, the children stopped playing their games and lined up single file around the room. They all stood still, smiling at him.

He had expected something a lot different, so their behavior unsettled him in a good way. He walked along the line, looking at each of the children without saying a word. Once he had perused all the merchandise, he turned to the man.

"I will take all of them!" he said. "They are fine merchandise, and you have looked after them very well. They will fetch a good price when I get them home. Prepare them to ship out."

It shocked the man again. This business was becoming quite a simple operation! He did not expect to sell all of them at one time. Now he was going to need to figure out what to tell the other clients.

He gave instructions to the staff to prepare the children, then he and the client went off to close the transaction. He breathed a sigh of relief. At least now, he would have some cash for his efforts!

As the children walked out of the barn, the dogs overwhelmed the dog master and broke free. They raced toward the children and the staff at full speed. The dog master called them back, but they did not listen.

Everyone, the staff, the man, and the clients all ran for cover! However, the children knew the truth, so they just laughed and ran to meet the dogs. As they met, each of the dogs flopped onto the ground, waiting for their reward. The children broke rank and ran screaming in excitement. They began patting the dogs and scratching their ears. Everyone was enjoying the event like it was a Sunday picnic! (Well, except for the adults, especially the dog master!)

At a later point, the chaos ended. The dogs sauntered off in one direction and the children walked down to the boat, entered their room, and sat down. It was as if they were going on a Sunday charter!

As the children looked back, the last thing they saw of the island were two groups. The first was a group of adults looking at each other in shock with one adult crying his eyes out, (guess who?), and the second group, a dozen lazy dogs flopped on the ground facing each other like they were having a chat!

As the boat pulled away, the man's mind was all jelly, but now at least he had a huge bag of money! It had all been worthwhile.

Unbeknownst to the captain of the ship, he had thirty-three extra passengers on board. Merle, Papi, Tarita, and the third group were all on board too!

Once they were out to open sea, Papi was off to do reconnaissance. She flitted about the boat from stem to stern, looking to see what she could see. She even let the crew see her. Several of them commented that it was odd to see a butterfly this far from shore. Papi laughed her little butterfly laugh and thought to herself, "Where have I heard that before?"

Tarita took charge of the children. This was an easy job as were entertained by thirty butterflies.

Merle prepared to visit the captain. Before she headed off, she thought for a few minutes about how she would make her appearance. (she was getting good at her acting skills as she got into the drama now that she could dress herself as she needed by choice!)

She turned up in the pilothouse. In fact, she turned up so fast she scared the captain. He had been focusing on setting the course for the ship on the computer, so was not expecting visitors. However, he was... by a mermaid!

The captain had never encountered a mermaid in all his years of running boats, but he had heard stories about them. They were always so beautiful, and they did not speak with their mouths.

He just stood there and stared! He did not know what to do or to think.

Merle remained silent for a few moments, just smiling at him as he became mesmerized by the situation. She spoke to him through their minds, giving him instructions to set an alternative course. Somewhere in the recesses of his mind, the captain recalled a similar situation that had happened to him a few years ago. He smiled to himself.

The client was sitting in his private room, enjoying his victory with a few of his staff. It was an easy voyage to their home port. They had nothing to do of importance since they had prepared everything beforehand. Their destination was a private port that had no authorities to bother them. Their buyers would be there waiting, so it would just be a quick handoff and the deed was done... or so they thought!

The client knew these waters well, and they were not all that far from the shore, so it was easy for him to determine where they were on the cruise. As he chatted with his crew, he looked outside.

He tore off up to the pilothouse. He was fuming! This was not the course back to his port.

He ripped open the door to the pilothouse and came to a grinding halt. He had never seen a mermaid before, either!

Merle had perched herself on a stool, sipping a virgin cocktail that the captain had provided for her. They were laughing together like old friends when the client burst in. They looked at him, then all three of them started laughing. The client forgot why he had needed to see the captain, so he sat down with them and joined in their conversation. Merle even offered him a virgin Mai Tai, which he accepted with no hesitation.

The port authorities had better be ready for Merle, Goose, and their friends. They now had one hundred children heading for them to process!

# Chapter 13

The man did not know what to think anymore. In years past, things had been so simple. One just had to find a bunch of available children, herd them up and deliver them. It was so easy!

He was used to cranky children and even ones who thought they could escape. Those were just part of the business. How things have changed now!

He really had a hard time getting his mind around how this last group had been so well-behaved. It really was quite disconcerting! However, times were changing, and these children were from an area where he had never collected before.

Time to think about the next phase. He had two clients who did not get their merchandise. They were not very happy when he told them they would have to wait for the next collection, but what could they do? He rubbed his hands together in joy, just thinking about how much extra money he was going to have once he had looked after these clients.

As soon as the boat carrying the last lot had departed from his port, he made three phone calls. The first two were to his clients who had not arrived yet, the third was to... Lindsay!

---

Goose and his cohorts were back at the Matrix already, having delivered their lot of children to the authorities when he received the phone call.

He called everyone together and told them the good news. "We have to go back. They have shipped all the children we collected out to their new lives.

He doesn't know they are on their way here. The first actual client showed up, liked all the children, and took them all. However, two more clients did not receive any goods. The man called Lindsay to find some more."

"We are going to have a very busy place around here once the first group of children arrives. What are we going to do when we collect more?" asked Condor.

"That is a good point. I will chat with Beth and Sheila before we take off. That will be up to them to make plans," said Goose. "I will also check in with Merle to find out how she and the rest are coming along."

The next morning, they were all sitting together in Lindsay's hotel room, ready to begin the next search. They needed to stall for a few days so that Merle and all the butterflies could join them, since they were still on the boat.

Shortly after breakfast, Lindsay's phone rang. Of course, it was the man. He wanted to meet later that morning. His clients were impatiently waiting for their cargo, which at this point did not even know their fate.

"We need to find out if he knows that I rescued all the children. That will make a tremendous difference in how he behaves!" said Lindsay. "He sounded upbeat on the phone, so I am guessing he doesn't. If so, we will have to create a stall tactic to let everyone catch up!"

Sure enough, when they met later in the morning, he was in a state of euphoria. He thought he owned the world now. It was quite funny, but also quite intolerable!

"I need you to go out today and get me another hundred. I can have the ship ready in two days. It is already sitting in the harbor," he told Lindsay. "I have my men ready and waiting. We won't even need to store them this time. As you collect them, we will just haul them straight to the boat."

Lindsay told him he had his men ready, and they would head out, but it was really going to depend on whether any more children were hiding in the area. He then reminded him they had already cleaned out one hundred children in the area not that long ago. Before the man could say any more, Lindsay got up to leave.

This irritated the man since he thought he was king, however, he realized there was little he could do as he needed Lindsay and his crew to get the job done.

When Lindsay got back to the room, he was feeling very concerned. They needed to have Merle and the butterflies here to help, but they needed to finish what they were currently doing.

"We just need to create a diversion," said Condor. "Something that will cause a sufficient delay. What can we come up with really quick?"

Raven then suggested, "There is only one road into the area where the fighting is occurring. There are several really tall derelict buildings along the way. We could check the area to ensure there is no one in the area, then do some demolition work!"

Condor then jumped in. "That would be easy enough to do, but he would find another way for us to get around the mess... unless... we were to get trapped in the rubble!"

Once the plan was in place, Lindsay contacted the man to let him know that they were heading into the area. He was going to stay behind to organize things from his side, but the others would be heading off shortly.

That afternoon, the man got the report about two large buildings collapsing near the entrance to the town. The main road into the area was completely blocked and would remain so for several days or more, depending on when the excavation equipment could clean up the mess.

Lindsay then phoned him back a while later, telling him that his crew was stuck inside one building that had collapsed. They had thought they heard children in the building, so they were searching it when it came down.

The man was fuming, but Lindsay assured him he was on top of it, but that it may take some time to get his men back to safety.

Just to add insult to injury, the next day, the man got a call from the head engineer on the ship. He told him that a problem had occurred in one of the engines. The ship would have to be drydocked for several days to make the repair.

"When it rains, it pours!" the man muttered to himself. "Now I have to make excuses to my clients. They are getting impatient."

---

Things had gone really well on the ship with Merle, Tarita, Papi, and the third group. Merle had gotten the captain to run the ship at full throttle so they could get to the harbor faster. She felt she needed to see this job through to the end just in case something unpredicted occurred. She also wanted to give everyone on board a bit of relaxation time before they headed back to work with Lindsay again.

The children had been a complete delight for Merle and her group. It really was like a school junket on the ship. The crew members, and even the client, were happily engaged in looking after the children, so all of her crew could just relax and enjoy the ride.

Once they reached the harbor, they immediately offloaded the children into the hands of the port authorities, the client and his men voluntarily gave themselves up for arrest, and all was well. They released the captain and the crew to go on their way.

Merle immediately contacted Beth to apprise her of the situation, then gathered the group to tell them they were going back to collect more children.

"Because this client took all the children, the man needs some more children to be collected right away. Lindsay and the Wind Surfers are already on the scene. They have created a diversion to give us some time to get there."

All the members of the third group were excited and ready to go. They really liked this new job. Along with the three ladies, they all headed off to their next mission. The third group headed back to the city where the circus was working, while the ladies immediately focused on landing in Lindsay's hotel room.

Lindsay smiled as they appeared before him. Not long after, all the Wind Surfers reappeared as well.

"Just like old times!" laughed Lindsay. "I will just have to get a larger room next time!"

"We are going to have to be extra vigilant this time. Who knows what kinds of traps this man is going to set for us this time," Goose said. "I am not all that fond of being gassed and trapped again. Once was more than enough!"

"Fortunately, we are not storing them this time. He wants to load them straight onto the boat. He wants us to call him when we have a lot, and he will send transportation," Lindsay said.

"I have a better idea," said Merle. "How about you tell him we can provide the transportation as well. That way, we can minimize his involvement."

That done, the hunt for the next lot of children began. They wanted to check out the local buildings again just to make sure they were clean. If they were, that meant getting closer to the fighting zone. If that were so, they would bring in the third group, but they would have to set up special provisions for them, so they stayed safe.

They had never been near a military action before, so did not know what went on.

Later, they met again in the hotel room. There were no children left in the area. They agreed that Mike, Tomas, and Goose would head over to the war zone to investigate the situation. In the meantime, the third group would join them in the hotel room. This was going to be one full room!

---

"The one thing on our side that we observed was that they only fight in the daytime, so hopefully we can get in and out in one evening," Mike reported. "I am glad our squad of butterflies are here now, so we can get in and out quickly."

"I think that our greatest danger is booby traps. We don't need another episode like what happened to Hummingbird!" Tomas added. "We need to create a method for seeing any traps, so we can do something about them."

"Physical traps on the ground will only be a problem if there are children behind the traps. It is the electronic ones I am concerned about. That last one packed a pretty big wallop," Tomas continued.

Then Goose suggested, "Let's manifest some special goggles for each member of the third group that will allow them to see electronic fields!"

And there it was! The solution!

Fifteen minutes later, the entire third group were fluttering off wearing their amazing new goggles! They could see normally, but had the added benefit that might just prove to be a lifesaver. They all laughed at each other, wearing goggles as they headed out. After all, whoever thought about butterflies wearing glasses before!

As the butterflies flew to the war zone, Goose drove the truck he had conjured up to a safe spot near the area. Merle rode in the front seat with him just in case they ran into anyone that wished to discuss their presence.

Sure enough, just as they were about to park, a soldier appeared out of nowhere. He pointed his rifle at them and yelled to stop. He had a very mean look on his face as he jabbed the rifle at them.

Once Goose had stopped the truck, Merle immediately jumped out and walked up to the man. This kind of knocked him off guard, partially because he did not expect a woman to be present, and second, because she dared to be unconcerned with his surliness.

Merle immediately started the conversation "We are here from an agency to protect any children that have been orphaned because of the war. We have no interest in your war!"

The soldier maintained his position with the rifle pointing at her. Merle walked right up to him, took hold of the barrel of the rifle, and pushed it downward, quietly saying "It is not polite to point that thing at people! Someone might get hurt!"

The soldier immediately pointed it at her again and fired... or at least tried to. He stood there in shock for a moment, but when he realized that Merle had squeezed the barrel flat as she had pushed it down. He turned tail and ran!

She got back in the truck, then said to Goose, "I was really hoping to have a friendly chat with him. Guess he did not like me ruining his gun!"

Goose then replied, "This might cause us a problem. We have been able to wander about unnoticed before. Now we are going to be the talk of the town, especially when he shows them his rifle."

Just then, the soldier reappeared. He laid his rifle down on the ground before them. Merle got back out of the truck and walked up to him. He immediately began to cry, so Merle took him in her arms and hugged him.

Merle could soon fill the butterflies in on everything she had learned about any traps and, more importantly, where the soldier thought there might be children hiding. At the end of their conversation, Merle told the soldier to go home to his family. The war was over for him.

---

The butterflies were flying all over the area in search of children. After a thorough search, they had found none. Fortunately, they had found no traps, either. They reconvened at the truck to rest and make new plans.

They still had not actually entered the war zone, mostly because they did not like the noise. If you think a cannon going off is loud for human ears, try to imagine what the sound would be like to a butterfly! It looked like they were going to have to get really, really tiny earplugs!

They all knew the success of this mission depended on them, so once they had rested and eaten, the butterflies took to the air again, this time into the war zone. They had heard all the racket earlier, so they had made note of where they thought the noise was being made. They all decided to try to stay away from that area. There were plenty of new buildings to check out in this quieter, unknown part of town.

Finally! After about thirty minutes of flying, they started hearing the noises they were in search of. Now to just home in on the noises!

Papi had joined the third group for this part of the mission. Her job was to stay above but near them, so that when they found children, she could convey the information back to Goose and Merle. They could then move the truck into the area.

Success came quickly. In fact, more than they could handle in the truck in one load. How were they going to handle this? They wanted to get the children out of the area as quickly as possible, but they would need to leave some of them where they could be safe, so they could retrieve them later.

Goose said, "there is an abandoned farmhouse a few miles from here. I recall seeing it when we drove to the port during the last project.

Let's take half of them there. They will be safe while we get the rest. We can feed them and get them ready for the next step of their journey while we take the remainder directly to the ship. "

The children were so mesmerized by the ensemble of butterflies that they forgot they were afraid. When they arrived at the farmhouse, they happily jumped off the truck and headed right into the house.

Tomas was already there, waiting for them inside. He had already checked the property out to make sure there were no surprises.

"I have already spoken with him. We can take them straight to the ship," Lindsay told Goose and Merle as they arrived back at the pickup site.

When they arrived at the dock, the boat was indeed ready for the first group. They had expected to see the man jumping up and down in elation, but he was not there. However, the first mate saw them arrive and came down to meet them.

"We will be back in a couple of hours with the final group," she told him as she jumped back into the front of the truck.

Later that night, the ship, with the man somewhere on board, headed off to the island. He had already contacted the two remaining clients to meet him there. He did not like the idea of having them meet, but he wanted to just do a straight transfer from one boat to the other so he could be done with this whole thing.

To break up the group of new children, he was going to auction them off right on the dock as they disembarked. He thought this would be a brilliant way of generating a little extra cash, but again, his plans never seem to quite come together the way he wanted.

When the ship docked at the island, the two clients were standing together on the island with suitcases of cash. As he walked off the ship, they handed him the suitcases.

"We will take it from here. Just take your money and buzz off. We will decide for ourselves which children will go where," the one client told him.

At first, he tried to take control of the situation, but then his brain kicked in and he realized he had already finished his part, so he took the briefcases and headed up to the house. Thirty minutes later, all three ships vanished into the vast abyss of the ocean.

Now, this presented a problem for the gang! They needed to be in two places at once. To complicate matters, the two ships were heading on the same course, so could see each other. If they commandeered one causing it to change course, the captain of the other ship would question this move. Both ships would have to be commandeered at the same time.

Have you ever heard that phrase, "You can't be in two places at once." That statement was about to be proved incorrect!

The children were fine on each of the boats. The butterflies realized what was happening, so they hid in children's coats as they entered the boat to find their assigned seat. The challenge was going to be for Merle and the other adults.

The weather had been quite calm this day. The sun had shined all day. Usually, that meant clear skies and calm seas at night. The captains were quite perplexed when suddenly a thick bank of fog settled in over them.

At the same moment, as the fog settled in, half of the Wind Surfers projected themselves onto each of the boats. They could now get their work done on the crew and the client, so they would no longer be a problem.

Merle waited for a bit to let the captains get their bearings in the fog and to calm down. This was another first-time trick for her, but she pulled it off. She projected herself into the bridge rooms of both boats at the same time!

Weren't those captains surprised when they turned to gaze upon a beautiful mermaid in their midst!

The port authorities would really be able to justify their jobs this month- almost 200 children to be processed!

The Matrix would be bursting at the seams by the time they processed and released all these children to them.

---

The man was a very happy person! (As happy as a person like him can be, anyway!) He had disposed of all the children. He had received more money for the work than he had hoped. He could now just relax and just do whatever his mind wanted.

He thought he might stay on the island for a while. After spending so much time in the war zone managing the capture of the children, he had quite had enough of people, period.

He sent home all but a few of the workers he had hired, so now he could have some peace and quiet.

One morning, a few days after the ships had left, he went for a walk. On the far side of the island, there was a beautiful sandy beach. Once he got there, he slipped off his shoes so he could let the sand sift between his toes. He even walked into the water just to feel the water slapping up against his legs.

He became so relaxed; he sat himself under a tree at the edge of the beach. The warm wind and the smell of the ocean were entrancing! He slipped off into a little catnap.

He dreamed. It was a dream he had never dreamed of having. It was a peaceful dream. It even had an angel. He relaxed more, and for the first time in his life, he felt content.

She said to him "*I am Rachel. I serve the Universal God that created this earth and all that exists. I invite you to join me in this moment of knowing yourself through the eyes of God.*"

It startled him for a moment that the angel actually had spoken to him, but then he was so relaxed, he just smiled back at her.

Rachel continued, *"You have done great service to mankind by collecting these children. It is through your efforts that the evolution of God's newest species of human has appeared on this beloved planet. We thank you. Be at peace."*

The dream ended as the angel faded away. He slept for a long time, not thinking about what she had said. When he finally awoke, he stretched and smiled at himself and embraced the wonderful life he was having at the moment.

He was feeling quite hungry, so he made his way back to the house. It amazed him how bright and beautiful the nature of the island appeared as he walked. He guessed that the sleep on the beach had been so good that it had heightened his eyesight. He felt so good!

When he arrived at the house, one worker prepared a scrumptious meal for him. They thought it kind of strange that the man actually was pleasant to them. He even laughed, something they had never heard him do before.

During the evening, he called the servants together. He handed them each a huge wad of cash, then dismissed them so they could return to their families.

Late that night, Rachel came to invite him to come home... and he accepted.

# Chapter 14

Things were a buzz at the Matrix. The whole place was crazy with excitement. Beth, Sheila, and the other staff had gotten so used to the quiet, they were not sure what it was going to be like soon. Mayhem was on the horizon!

Merle, Tarita, Papi, the Wind Surfers, and the third group were all due to reappear (literally) as soon as the boats tied up at the Port Authority docks. Lindsay was in flight and was due the next day.

Fortunately, the rescued children were still in the hands of the immigration people. They would remain there until the authorities could release them to arrive in about one month. There was a lot to be done before they showed up, so there was no time to waste!

In the next few months, the staff would have to receive, settle, and begin retraining about 200 children!

Never in their wildest dreams had any of the people who made up the lifeblood of the Matrix ever thought that they would ever house close to three hundred people at one time in their home. However, such was about to be the case!

It was very fortunate that early upon Merle's arrival at the Matrix, she had manifested a completely new wing to the complex as a gift for her birthing. Until now, the ell had been vacant.

"It is going to be tight, but I think we can fit them all in," Beth said to everyone. They were all now back from their journeys, so this was the first official get-together. The meetings were different now.

In fact, it was more like a convention, since the accepted policy for major decision-making and announcements included all residents and invited members.

Even though there was very serious business to be conducted, the meeting had an air of joy to it.

"We now have a small army of peaceful soldiers to prepare, so we can begin our real work. We have finished collecting kidnapped children at this point since our collector has opted to return home.

Our true mission is the spiritual education of human beings. Life has provided us with lessons in the past for the evolution of the souls of human beings that have now become redundant. We, as members of humanity, have repeated them for centuries with not enough growth.

Now it is our job to offer new lessons that will assist humans to become more connected to Source. Rachel will assist us in creating new events as well as assisting many of us to take on new roles within society, outside of the general affairs of the Matrix."

Everyone sat silently, pondering what Beth had just told them. It was a little unsettling for many of them as, like all humans, there is comfort in familiarity. There is also excitement in change!

This was Lindsay's opportunity to announce his big news. There was a group based in their town that had been formed after the Matrix had successfully beaten a lawsuit by some very unhappy people who did not get their merchandise.

Lindsay told his story "When I arrived at our airport, four people were standing at the arrivals entrance behind a placard bearing my name. I was quite nervous as I walked toward them, but they immediately called me by name and smiled like I was some kind of hero.

I understand this group evolved from the efforts of the Matrix. When they heard I had pitched in to help bring the children home, they had a meeting and unanimously agreed that I needed to join with them. So congratulate me as the fifth member of The Children's Advocacy Group!" Lindsay grinned from ear to ear as everyone stood up and cheered for him. The Wind Surfers started dancing around, hollering his name and whooping like a bunch of crazed soccer fans.

When the crowd finally settled down, Goose stood up and looked at Lindsay. Smiling, he said, "We already knew, because we are joining you!"

Again the crowd went crazy and for the first time ever, Lindsay joined the Wind Surfers in the mayhem.

"At first, we will split our time between the Matrix and the Advocacy Group," said Goose. "We are needed here as well since there will be hundreds of new mouths to feed and retrain soon! We have about one month before they will arrive, so that will give us some time to get the feel of the Advocacy Group and where we can go with it. I have a feeling we are going to be busy for a very long time!"

Tarita then stood up, and in her quiet butterfly-like manner added her voice to the excitement, "We have an enormous flock of butterflies in our midst that are planning to contribute to our next phase as well. Although most of the folks in group three I am sure would love to continue with their life at the circus, we have some other activities in mind for them, at least for most of the time!"

Papi beamed as she listened to her mentor. All of group three sat quietly, waiting for Tarita to continue.

"Being that we are butterflies, the most noble of insects, we are going to become Environmental Advocates... but in a very special way. We are going to fly in search of places where the pollution has caused a serious reduction in all insects, especially our friends, the honey bees. Once we can identify what is causing the problem, and gain enough evidence to prove the source, we will turn the evidence over to Merle, who will advocate for change."

Merle then continued from Tarita, saying "I have connected with an Environmental Advocacy Group who has good connections into the Ministry of Environment but have had a great deal of difficulty getting proof because they can't get close enough to the issues. They do not know how we are going to collect the information, however, they have heard about the work we have done in rescuing children in rather unorthodox ways, so they are open to seeing what we can do."

Again, the meeting went sideways as the Wind Surfers, Lindsay, Tarita, Papi, and Merle all went crazy dancing around and celebrating. Finally, Beth, Teesha, and Sheila gave in and joined them! They did not conclude the meeting! Well, actually it concluded in what was becoming the usual ending... party time... break out the instruments, Wind Surfers!

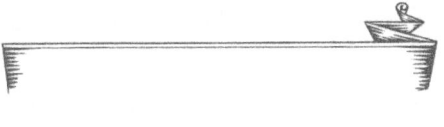

# Chapter 15

P api woke up with a start. The noise actually threw her out of bed. It sounded like firecrackers going off in a 45-gallon drum. So much for any more sleep tonight!

Knowing this was not just a noisy dream, Papi climbed back into the dream. She needed to find out who or what needed her attention! What a way to wake up!

The steel drum was standing out in a field. It looked like it was raining cats and dogs, as the saying goes, except the raindrops were too big. Papi cringed as she realized those raindrops were bees. They were crashing into the barrel as they died... screaming.

It seemed like a painful death for these beautiful creatures.

Even though it was the middle of the night, Papi tore out of bed. She needed to talk with Tarita. The bees need their help!

---

Tarita was already awake. She had the same dream. Still groggy from the sudden awakening, they both almost crashed into each other in the hallway.

"What is happening with our friends? It looked like a mass suicide, Tarita," Papi sobbed.

"One thing that sets the animal kingdom apart from humans is that they do not kill themselves. Unlike our plant friends who have evolved high enough spiritually to be willing and able to step aside, animals do not do that. No, something is killing them, and it must be really bad if it forced them to project this dream to us. Let's see what we can find out," Tarita replied as she gave her beloved Papi a consoling hug.

They sat together on a yoga mat, going straight into a meditation. Soon, they reached out to the bee diva, the highest consciousness of the bee kingdom.

Usually, when one approaches a diva, the energy lifts the applicant to an almost unbearable energy level since the diva is the accumulated consciousness of all their species. However, things were not that way today.

Papi and Tarita saw before them a broken diva. She looked like she had fought a horrific war, and lost. She lay before them, sobbing for her beloved bees.

Rachel immediately appeared with them. She took a deep angel breath, holding it for a bit, then blew it right into the bee diva's face. She instantly returned to her glory. Rachel then disappeared.

"We are doomed," she said sadly. "We cannot continue to do our work, or even exist anymore because of all the actions that humans have chosen to perpetrate that have affected our environment. Our species and many others of the insect domain are dropping dead even as they fly. If this problem continues, humans, themselves will cease to exist on this plane."

The diva broke down and cried. Papi and Tarita knew she spoke the truth. They needed to do something before it was too late.

---

Mike was sitting, having his breakfast when they walked in. He could see they had something urgent on their mind. They sat down and immediately launched into their concerns.

"Let's figure this out and get on it quick. I think the first thing we need to do is survey the situation so we can make an action plan, and that is Merle's territory, so..." And with that, Mike and Merle traded places.

Sitting in the yoga room, they formed a triangle by holding hands. As they focused on their breaths, they called the bee diva to join them so they could see the problem clearly.

As they sat, the bee diva showed them pictures of field after field of grain, or at least a semblance of grain. It had been genetically modified so much, it hardly looked like the original plant, and the grain plants were crying tears that flowed down over the toxic chemicals that prevented them from receiving the sun's rays to help them flourish.

Then, they swooped over to a bushy area nearby. There were signs that someone posted, stating that they had sprayed toxic chemicals on all the plants in the area, because of one species the people feared. Where they were not sprayed, the plants had been mowed down, right before the flowers were ready to pop their pretty little heads out.

They were not finished yet, but they truly wished they were, because they were all feeling very nauseous by now... and angry. It just went on and on, from farmers using ammonia for fertilizer that killed the worms in the soil, to spraying massive amounts of pesticides and herbicides on plants that just thrive on love.

"The plants just do not stand a chance, so neither did the bees... or the mosquitoes... or the butterflies," the bee diva said.

"Doesn't mankind understand the meaning of symbiotic relationships? Can't they understand that plants only exist because they have a specific job to do at that time? Don't they understand that when the job is done, they will disappear on their own? Those poor Scotch Brooms are just trying to repair the soil that got turned over when the farmer accidentally plowed into that gravel bank.

If the plants don't grow and mature, if the bees and butterflies can't pollinate the plants, if the mosquitoes don't populate adequately, nothing can exist. The very basic building blocks of life on earth are undermined.

The plants need to exist to grow and reproduce. They need the bees and butterflies to pollinate them. The bees need the pollen from the flowers for nectar so they can have nourishment. The birds need the insects for food, so they can help carry off seeds to replenish the plant world.

If this process fails, so does life on earth... including human life. And yet!!! It is the choices that humans are consciously making that are completely to blame for this catastrophe!"

As the bee diva finished, they opened their eyes to the yoga room. They knew this was one of the most important projects they could ever be involved in.

They also realized they were not alone!

"We want to help too!" all the members of the third group cried in unison. "The insects are our friends as well." This was especially true since every one of these people could transition into butterflies at the flap of a wing! (a fact that Papi is especially proud of!)

So, a plan that now included, not three, but thirty-three people (or butterflies) came to light. For the first time in a very long time, the bee diva smiled as she watched the plan unfold.

The first thing that needed to happen was to stop the unnecessary deaths. There was little point in fixing the problem if there were no insects left. Rachel came to help at this point. Who else could provide mini-gas masks for millions of beautiful creatures?

If one was able to hear at the right level, as our people can, you would hear millions of giggling voices as the insects found themselves flying about trying to do their duties with life-saving masks on their faces.

That took care of the most urgent problem, however, they were not out of the woods yet, so to speak. They could still suffer from malnutrition and skin absorption. The best temporary solution was to get them out of there until things could be corrected to an acceptable level.

Rachel again did her own brand of magic. A large natural area with forests, hills, meadows, and a lovely little creek appeared before them. They all smiled as they sniffed in the scents of the pine and cedar trees, the beauty of all the phlox, lupines, and roses as they swayed in the gentle breeze. They almost forgot the project at hand as the sound of a little waterfall crept into their ears as the water in the creek made its way.

As soon as the refuge had manifested, every insect headed in that direction. Most of them made it there safely, but sadly many succumbed to the poisons so thoughtlessly thrown about by people. Now, at least, there was hope for the survival of these species!

Special rain began to fall on the insects. They needed to be cleansed of any poisons that clung to their skin. Can you imagine millions of insects bathing together? Good thing they did not need shampoo!

The final step before work could begin on the problem was food for the insects. Rachel waved her wand over the entire area. Little particles of food floated down from high in the sky. Manna for insects! They were just exactly what each insect needed for the interim! Phew!!!

For this project, even Merle became a butterfly again. She only took a minute to reminisce of her butterfly experience earlier as she was being born. So, all thirty-three butterflies, properly outfitted with gas masks headed off to put an end to this blight.

It was not long before a farmer appeared before them busy plowing his fields, injecting ammonium nitrate into the furrows. If only he could hear what these butterflies said as he came into view. As the fertilizer soaked in, the worms either dug themselves in deeper or died on the spot.

It would have been nice if they could just turn the solution into water, but that was not how this had to play out. They needed the farmer to learn the hard way. The butterflies pulled together forming one gigantic butterfly, then flew right in front of the farmer's face. He was so shaken by the action, that he momentarily lost focus of his work. This allowed the spray injector hose to bounce out of the ground and sprayed him right in the face. The farmer fell to the ground. Fortunately for him, the tractor missed him as it continued on to its final resting spot... deep in a swamp.

The farmer lay on the ground gasping for air, his face contorted from the pain of the chemical burning his skin and eyes. Finally, he lost consciousness. As he lay there, the huge butterfly landed on him. Collectively, they projected love to the man. It took a long time for it to cause any sensation, but eventually, he stirred. When he opened his eyes, the butterfly was sitting on his chest looking straight at him. The butterfly smiled, and he realized. The farmer never used ammonium nitrate again.

This was only one farmer though. Thousands were still polluting the earth, killing off the worms and the soil. After the farmer had healed, he knew he needed to make amends. He had never realized before that the short-term gain of chemical fertilizers was a long-term loss for Mother Nature.

The farmer turned over the farm to his children when they promised to only farm in accordance with nature, and went off. He had a new mission! He walked with a new gait, too. His life now had purpose.

He visited his elected officials. He visited the granaries. He visited anyone who would listen. Eventually, after much ridicule and many threats, he was invited to an interview on a television show.

The TV announcers were determined to discredit him and send him packing back to his farm, but he was on a mission to save his world. He shone like a star in the interview. Soon, all the networks were scrambling for him. He was a national sensation.

The major coup occurred when the chemical companies sued him. They were going to take him for millions. That would shut up his tree-hugger message. They were in business to make money, lots of money. They were not going to let his whimpering spoil their agenda.

However...

Because of the severity of the situation, the courts suspended all other cases and placed this case first in the highest court of the land. The chemical guys were elated. The sooner they shut this guy up, the sooner they could get back to killing worms. Who needed worms, anyway? Plows are better and faster at busting up the soil.

However...

The judge was not in the least sympathetic to their cause. He called it economic suicide. Maybe the chemical companies would benefit in the short-term, however, in the long-term, when there was no soil left, there would also be no economy... or food for people to enjoy.

The judge had previously examined all the evidence that the farmer had collected regarding the problem and had already decided on the verdict before taking his chair. The trial lasted long enough for the judge to mete out the highest penalties possible to the soon-to-be bankrupt chemical companies.

Smaller companies who had developed safer and more natural fertilizers and soil amendments flourished, especially after the judge ruled that the officers of these companies were required to ensure that no directors of these new generation companies could have their histories traced back to a now-bankrupt chemical company.

A second significant thing happened as well! The chemical companies had also been the manufacturers of the pesticides that were being sprayed on the plants near the forest. This did not eradicate the problem, but it sure took a bite out of it.

The butterflies all wondered in unison, as they looked at the continuing devastation when people would understand there are no plants that need to be eradicated! God creates nothing without a purpose!

After the farmer's victory, people who were plant-friendly began lobbying their politicians. Change was their byword! It took quite a long time but eventually, the government experts were enlightened. Look for the reason the plant is there, instead of poisoning it! Japanese knotweed is a calcium fixer. Build up the calcium so it will stay at acceptable levels and this beloved plant will move on without man's interference. What else can the plant kingdom tell us?

The bee diva was feeling like herself again. Soon, her bees could begin their work again... without gas masks!

The Matrix entourage held a meditation near the farmer's house. They wanted to feel the energy in the area to determine if they had cleaned everything up before all the bees returned. They were under pressure now, as the plants were missing their little friends, and spring was just around the corner.

As they tuned into the energies, they took a big sigh of relief. It did indeed feel much better now that the chemicals were gone. It would likely take a very long time for the land to heal, but with a little help...

Papi led a healing visualization. "Focus the energy of the sun wafting down into the earth. This energy is flowing into every particle of earth, causing any of the chemical residue to evaporate. Let the sunrays flow deep into the earth, letting every bit of unnatural chemicals be released from the soil.

Now, take a deep breath, hold it for a minute, then blow the positive energy into the soil, causing it to be healed. See the vitality of the soil radiate in good health. Hold the vision for a few moments to embed it in the energetic nature of the soil.

Take one more big deep breath, hold it, and let go. The soil is now healed. The chemical residue has been released and returned to the Universe to be recreated for good. All is well."

As quick as they opened their eyes, Rachel reached down and scooped up all the evaporated chemical residue and sent it off to the Universe for recycling.

As they peered down into the soil, they saw the earthworms were rushing back up into the topsoil. The worms waved to them in thanks (which was really tricky because worms do not have hands).

"Are we done now?" asked one of the third group."

Papi let herself flow into the energies of the area again to ensure everything was good. At first, she smiled, then her lips turned down.

"As long as I stay focused on the soil and earth energy, all is well, but my sense is that there is still something wrong, very wrong. I do not know what it is, but there is a frequency that just does not feel healthy," said Papi.

"It is in the air!" exclaimed Tarita. "We have been so busy focusing on the earth, we have forgotten to be inclusive. The air carries so much invisible energy, it is easy to miss looking there too."

Everyone turned on their night vision so they could see the activity in the air. The trees were shaking from the energetic activity that they breathed in. They were constantly being stimulated, so they could not relax and just be.

"We need to fix this too, then. If it is bothering the trees, it will definitely be harmful to the insects and birds. Let's see if we can figure out what is causing the vibration."

Focusing in on the vibration, they set flight. They wanted to physically find the source.

It took a while, but eventually, they saw a vast forest of tall towers ahead. They did not know what they were at first, but there were hundreds of them. There was no energy emitting from them, but there was definitely something that did not feel right.

Merle pushed into her memory banks, trying to get a grasp on what these towers were. She was definitely not familiar with them. They just stood there, with their propellers turning and turning in the breeze. They did not seem to be a problem, and yet, this is where they were led to.

They tuned into the towers again to see if they could get a grasp on the situation. What is causing an issue here?

"It is the frequency emitted by the speed the blades are turning!" screamed Papi. "It does not seem to bother us, but it is just the right frequency to be harmful to the insects and the birds."

They were right, the propellers were set to turn and turn, all day long. They emitted an uncomfortable frequency just from the rotations.

They looked around to see if they could figure out how to fix this situation. They could temporarily shut down the towers, but they knew the men at the site would quickly start them up again. No, there had to be a long-term solution.

The men at the site! Of course, that was the answer. Merle quickly started trying to access the minds of any one of them for an answer. She could not get in. They needed to get their attention.

"Rather than forming a single giant butterfly, let's head to the area where they are working and put on a show for them. All we need is to get their attention for a moment, then I can get into their minds!" Merle exclaimed.

Flying in formation, thirty-three butterflies put on a mini airshow for the men below. They flew straight in one behind the other, almost getting caught in the hair of one man, they flew so close. These butterflies were skilled acrobats, though, so close was good. It got their attention.

They flew up high into the sky forming a big circle, looking like a Ferris Wheel rotating round and around. That got the men's attention! They dropped what they were doing and stared at the show. They did not know butterflies could be so entertaining.

Now Merle had the opening she needed. She focused on the consciousness of each man until she found the one that she needed.

This man understood how these things worked, therefore; he knew the answer to the problem. Now she just needed to figure out how to get him to understand.

Tarita had the answer. She projected energy to him, just like she had previously done up in the Arctic. The man was now putty for Merle. She focused on his mind, creating a psychic room for them to meet.

He was a little flustered when he found himself sitting in the room with Merle, but she smiled at him, and he relaxed. He was a pretty down-to-earth kind of person, so it was a little unsettling to be chatting with someone in a room in his head.

"Hi Don, I am reaching out to you today because we need your help. It seems that these windmills you are working on are creating havoc for the birds and the insects in this area. Are you aware of this?"

"I have seen some reports as such, but I do not understand what they are referring to. As long as they don't fly too close to the blades they won't get hurt," he replied.

"The problem is not with the blades, Don. The problem is the frequency of vibration caused by the wind turbulence from the windmills. It hurts their hearing and can be uncomfortable in their bodies."

"Birds and insects can hear? They have feelings? Really! Who would have thought! I guess it is a consequence of progress. Nothing is perfect," he replied.

"Do you understand the building blocks of our ecology, Don?" Merle asked. He just looked like she had spoken Spanish to him. No entiendo.

"The bees and other insects form the basis of our food chain. They pollinate the flowers on fruit trees and all the vegetable plants that give us our food. The bees are dying faster than they can reproduce due to chemical and electromagnetic pollution. If we do not change our ways, we will die of starvation in the not very distant future."

She sat quiet for a few moments, allowing what she had said to sink in. Then she continued.

"Don, we need to come up with a way to break the disruptions these windmills are causing, so the insects can survive and flourish. We don't need to stop these machines; we just need the frequency to change or be disrupted."

Don thought for a minute. Then said, "That is not difficult. All we have to do is reprogram them to change speeds periodically, to change the frequency. I will do that today on all our farms, and I will reach out to the community to join in. Thank you for bringing this concern to me."

As soon as Merle and Don closed their meeting, Don went into the instrument room. Within hours, the frequency was noticeably different. The bees and all their friends sighed a breath of relief.

Just in time for spring!

# Chapter 16

Tarita slept soundly, dreaming about nothing in particular... until... the drumming started. Tomas and Tarita had become so comfortable with their unique life that it no longer matters which expression was visible at bedtime. Sleep was never difficult, no matter what, except tonight.

As she continued in her slumber, the drumming became louder and more intense. It soon became so loud it woke her up, but as she opened her eyes, she realized that the drumming was not coming from the outer world, it was coming from her dream.

Tarita relaxed and slipped back into a sound sleep. No drumming! Just wonderful sleep.

She never mentioned the drumming to anyone the next day. She just shrugged it off as she got on with her duties. That night, though, the drumming happened again.

Soon, the dreams became more real. She began seeing the drummer... and dancers. The music was very hypnotic. Tarita could feel herself being pulled into the music. The music frightened her.

Tarita forced herself back from the music, and awake. She was not going to fall into that trap!

She never slept for the rest of the night. She was feeling too shaken! She could hardly wait until morning.

At breakfast, she sought Mike. He listened intently, looking very concerned.

"We had better figure out what this is about. Obviously, there is a reason for this dream to continue night after night. It is a good thing you were able to pull yourself back out."

Just as they were finishing their conversation, Lindsay appeared at the cafeteria door. He looked very concerned. As he sat down, he launched right into his reason for showing up today.

"We have received a message that we are very concerned about, so I wanted to get your take on it. It seems there is a group of Satanists that are using underground caves. The reports we are receiving claim they are kidnapping children and possibly sacrificing them. It seems they lure the children away from their parents, then hypnotize them through music and dance.

As soon as we heard about it, we checked the police reports in the area where they are believed to exist to see if any children are missing... there are about one hundred!"

Tarita groaned. She could hear the music again. It was trying to seduce her back into the dance. Mike could see she was struggling, so he took her hands calmly to keep her present. This worked for a few minutes until Mike felt himself being pulled in. The more he resisted, the deeper he fell into the abyss of the music.

Instantly, Rachel appeared, swishing her wand over the pair, forming a box of golden light surrounding them. They relaxed, looking at her in complete amazement.

"We have our work cut out for us with this group!" Rachel stated. "I have been aware of them for a while, but it has only been recently they have been increasing their activities. It is time for us to get to work!"

"But why are they trying to pull me in?" asked Tarita. "I am not a child."

"I suspect, it is because the music is similar to the early native drumming performed by the Yanomami people of your native

Venezuela. They beat their drums in very hypnotic rhythms to subdue their enemies," Rachel said.

Lindsay offered what he knew about the situation, then headed back to the Advocacy office so he could advise the others. This situation needed to be dealt with now!

Tarita was ready to head right off to the location where the children were missing. She was angry! Mike, or rather Merle, by now, retained a calmer perspective, so she took her friend by the shoulder and pushed her back into her chair.

"We need to get ourselves grounded and raise our energy really high to manage these. I am not sure what we need to do, so I vote we make some plans that will both protect us and disengage them. These are not ordinary people we are dealing with, my friend."

"One thing we need to know is how the warriors protected themselves from being hypnotized by the music. I think we should meditate on this for a bit. Let's head outside so the cedar trees can help us."

As they headed out to the forest, Merle glanced at the wing of the Matrix. It was being prepared for the new arrivals, but there should be no one in there at the moment.

However, as she stared through the windows, she could see people moving around inside. She nudged Tarita and pointed at the building.

They both headed in to find out who was in there... and received a very pleasant surprise... a woman sitting in lotus position floated in the air! She smiled radiantly at the two ladies and motioned for them to enter.

As Merle and Tarita stepped in, several other beings came into sight. They stood tall; however, their feet did not touch the ground. They hovered comfortably around the lady. The energy was radiant!

They stood quietly, calmly observing their new guests. A voice spoke softly in their minds, saying: "We are Pleiadeans. I am called

Lizu. Merle and Marita, we have long observed you, and are proud to come to your aid. We heard there was an issue that might need our assistance to heal, so we have made use of this area to organize ourselves and to make ourselves of service to you. The people you are about to interact with will require a special level of healing energy that our bodies are capable of transmitting."

At that moment, Rachel appeared. "There is a tremendous negative force that will have to be transitioned with the people we are investigating. My friends have agreed to help." And at that, Rachel swooped her arms lovingly to the Pleiadeans, welcoming them.

Merle and Tarita moved into the sitting room. They could feel their energy rising to match their guests. Suddenly, they found themselves floating with the others. They both laughed like little schoolgirls as they bobbed in the air. The Pleiadeans thought it was pretty funny too, so they let themselves go. Pretty soon everyone was bobbing around in the air, turning circles and bouncing off walls, even Rachel!

The room became very warm as the Pleiadeans raised their energies in concert to welcome the ladies. Then everyone settled down to business.

"We have never experienced the level of negative energy emanating from any group ever before. We suspect there may be a machine involved that emits discordant ultra-low frequency energy. It allows their egos to take full charge of their mind, with no limitations. They become hypnotized into believing that they are free to do as they please without repercussions," Rachel began.

"Do you have any idea where this machine might be found, Rachel?" enquired Tarita.

"We do not have a clear location yet; it seems to be in a different location each time we perceive it. It may not even be a machine. It is something we have never come across before. We definitely need to get to the bottom of this!"

"What do you know about these people, Rachel? Are they earthlings? Why do they sacrifice children?" Marita questioned anxiously.

"We will download what information we have about them into your minds when we meditate next. I will say though, that we suspect they are from elsewhere. That is why we felt our friends should join in on the project. The most important thing we can do right now is to ensure that we keep our energies as high as possible while remaining grounded in Universal Love."

"Should we be discussing this matter with the others, so they are aware of the situation?" asked Merle.

"I suggest you do not speak of this outside of this room. If anyone else has heard the drumming, then they are to be included, however, the others cannot see our friends, so they will not even know anything is going on. Lindsay and his group have had their minds redirected to other business until we conclude this matter. At this point, only you ladies will participate... and your male counterparts as well when needed."

At that, Rachel smiled and disappeared. Merle and Tarita returned to the forest to meditate. Only now, they had a lot more to ponder.

Once they found their favorite spots, they relaxed as best they could. The cedar trees knew they were feeling upset, so they lowered their boughs to give them a reassuring hug. They knew things would be okay.

As they moved into their meditations, they could see the information downloading into their minds. Now, at least, they would have something to help them figure out what they were up against. They were glad for their guests!

As they settled into the meditations, Rachel and Lizu joined them, taking them by the hands, so they formed a circle. As they stood, they began moving rhythmically in a circle. They each began deep positive breathing simultaneously while focusing on their solar plexus. The energies soared!

Merle and Tarita had never felt so much a part of the Cosmic. All they could feel was love-exaltation! Eventually, they became so immersed in the energy they lost singular consciousness, becoming one with all.

Higher and higher they ascended as they became One with Source- the ultimate goal of human consciousness.

Time ceased to exist as Merle and Tarita let themselves expand and expand.

Finally, with one last breath, they returned to consciousness, then into their bodies as they relaxed with their friends, the cedar trees. As they become more conscious of themselves, they realized something was different. They relaxed in the calm as they explored themselves, trying to figure out what had happened to make them feel so different.

Rachel and Lizu then appeared before them again.

"The feelings you are exploring are real. You are correct about the feeling that something has changed." Rachel said. "We have raised your energies to a new level, equal to those of the Pleiadeans. From this time forward, you are both fully integrated into one complete being. You are no longer Mike and Merle or Tomas and Tarita."

Looking at Merle, she said, "As a singular being, your name is now Oona, which means The One."

Then turning to Tarita, she said "You are the integrated twin, you will now be named Tan."

"These names are your soul names. These names have always been your singular identification here on earth and elsewhere, throughout your many incarnations. The names that identify you in the Akashic Records. They are your last connection to life in the mundane world."

"With these new names comes new abilities, and new responsibilities. Because you are so used to being at the high levels of consciousness, you may never consciously realize the difference. The vibration you now work at allows you complete access to the highest levels of Cosmic Consciousness. You may return at any time to your physical being and operate as your former selves as needed. However, your levels of operation are significantly higher."

"When you interact with others, such as with your people at the Matrix and any other humans, they will see you in whichever aspect you choose, but please understand your true work will be beyond their ability to comprehend. You will need to communicate at their level."

# Chapter 17

"We will look after your children until times are better. Just let us have them to take care of and you can focus on making your life better," the woman from the agency told the distraught parents.

Times were tough. No one had ever seen times like the present. The economy had completely crashed. There were no jobs to be had. The banks would like to repossess their homes, but they did not want them left empty.

To add to the ongoing problems, a drought had struck the area over one year ago, so nothing grew in the fields that were normally filled with corn, wheat, and other staples. The government emergency services were called to help but were too busy elsewhere so did not have the staff available to help the locals sort out their lives. They were starving. They were angry.

The only help was an agency who claimed to be able to take the children from the parents. They could take care of their young ones and feed them until times were better. Reluctantly, the parents let go of their little ones, not knowing they would likely never see them again.

---

"Throw those children in that room over there!" the people from the agency were told as they herded the children through the door of the abandoned school gym.

"Don't worry about them, just bring more," they were told. "Bring every child you can get your hands on. Tell the parents whatever you need to get them to give them to you, or else you will be joining them!"

The people recruited to collect children constantly heard the voice but did not know where it was coming from. They saw no one. It was just a voice, a terrifying voice.

They had seen other people who did not comply, but they never saw them again after they had refused. It was rumored something, or someone had killed them. No one knew for sure.

They were all so hungry. They were willing to do anything just to survive, so they did whatever they had to do. At the end of the day, they received a bowl of some tasteless gruel. It was more than the children received, for they received nothing, not even water.

They all heard the drumming. It was a hypnotic beat that went on forever. The drumbeat lulled them into a robotic state. They just did what they were instructed without complaining, or even thinking. On and on, the drumbeat rolled.

––––––––––––––––––

Tan could still hear the drumbeat, but now, thanks to the Pleiadeans, she could resist its hypnotic pull. In fact, she had been waiting for it to begin again. She was going to find where it was coming from. She was awake when the drumbeat began again. In fact, she had been calling it, trying to reconnect. Now she had it.

Oona was ready, too. They were determined they were going to find the source and do whatever needed to be done. Now was the opportunity they had been waiting for. Tan could hear the drum, so she prepared to project herself to it. Oona, not hearing it, connected her consciousness with her friend's mind. Together, they let themselves be absorbed into the source of the disturbance.

When they opened their eyes, they found themselves sitting in the same place as before. Astounded, they tried again and again... with the same result. They were going nowhere fast!

Lizu has been watching them telepathically. When they had stopped trying, she appeared before them. Without a word, the three of them tried the projection again... but failed again.

Rachel then appeared, looking perplexed. "You are doing everything right, so you should be able to project to the source of the drumbeat, but you remain right here. My suspicion is that the sound does not exist in the physical plane, therefore there is nowhere for you to project to."

"Something has to be causing it though, even if it does not have a physical presence," offered Oona. "Can we trust that we could allow ourselves to become entranced by it so we can find out what it would do to us, but still maintain enough of our minds to not be consumed by it?"

Lizu suggested, "If we have our Pleiadean members connect to your consciousness, then you let yourselves be pulled in, they can pull you back once we know what we need. This is risky though because we just do not know what we are up against."

Tan tried again, just letting herself be pulled away. Oona held her hand so she could be with her. Quickly they disappeared. The drumbeat got louder and louder as they traveled through space, through consciousness. All of a sudden, they felt themselves being pulled back.

They opened their eyes and found themselves sitting in front of Lizu and Rachel.

"We saw you being pulled into a time warp that we would not have been able to pull you back from had you gone any further. This is not the right method either," Lizu muttered.

"Let's have some Destiny Tea and see if it can help us see things more clearly," suggested Tan, and instantly cups of the hot, delicious tea were in their hands.

"Aha! I have it," exclaimed Oona. "Let's just go to the area and have a look around. Maybe we can discover why the people are feeling so negative. Then we can work backward from there!"

---

"Oh my! This area is supposed to be really fertile. We should be looking at fields of grains and orchards of apple trees. Something is really wrong here, and we need to find out what is causing this weather situation," said Tan.

"Let's see if we can find out anything from any of the locals. That way we can get a feel for the situation here as well," Oona suggested, as she headed toward a group of people.

As they approached the group, they both instantly could feel their energy drop, so they stopped and concentrated on recharging themselves.

"What do you want?" a middle-aged man snarled at the women as they approached. "We have had enough of strangers around here!" And at that, he turned back into the group, leaving Oona and Tan standing like they were not even there.

Oona then closed her eyes and focused on the man's mind, both soothing him and searching for the reason for his contempt. In seconds it was clear these were parents who had lost their children. They now had a doorway!

Moving further away from the group, they found a bench to sit on. While Oona kept her focus on this man's mind, Tan scanned the area for anything that did not feel right.

Oona saw herself sitting in a room chatting with the man. He cried in frustration as he told her how things had gone from a wonderful life with his wife and children working the family grain farm. The crops were just about ready to be harvested when things changed, almost like someone had flipped a switch. One day the fields were ready for harvest, the next day, the crops were dead. Not just his farm, but every farm for miles was in ruins.

They called the government agricultural people in. They also checked with the weather people. There was nothing to explain why the crops had failed. This was only the beginning!

The banks immediately flagged everyone in the region, causing their bank accounts and credit to be frozen. They could not even buy food unless they had cash!

Even the stores were affected, so, before long, food supplies began to dwindle. They reached out to the government for help but only found a deaf ear except for this one agency. They could not offer any real help except to lighten their burden by taking their children off their hands.

They said they would take care of them so they could focus on the bigger problems. Reluctantly, parents began releasing their children to these people, never seeing their children again.

At first, they were thankful for these people, who seemed to care about them and the situation, but eventually, they began to feel there was something not quite right. When they approached anyone from the agency, they got nowhere. These people only knew they needed to continue collecting children to get fed.

When they tried to find out where the children had been taken, they got nowhere. They tried to follow the agents but were blocked by armed guards.

It was no wonder these people were angry and wary of strangers!

---

Tan had found something of interest in her investigations. The drumbeats had started again. Rather than allowing herself to be hypnotized by them, this time she searched for the source. By focusing on the frequency of the beats, she could determine that they were not of natural cause. It was likely some kind of a machine.

She tried to focus on the location of the machine but had no luck, it just seemed to be everywhere!

------

Lizu and Rachel appeared before them. There had to be an answer. Maybe a fresh take on this would help.

"Let's take a bigger picture of the situation," Lizu suggested. "Let's project a few miles into space and look down at the affected area. That might give us a clue."

From this upper vantage point, the four focused on different levels of perception. Rachel focused on the astral level, searching the heavens for any source, while Lizu looked at the weather patterns of the region and any geological shifts. Oona scanned the earth itself, looking for any hidden secrets. Tan searched on the human level, searching for strangers to the area.

Whoever or whatever had created this situation certainly was a master at their craft! There just seemed to be nothing out of place, until.... Oona saw it!

As she focused on the ground itself, she let her mind flow down into the depths of the earth. For the first while, everything looked normal, then she started to find resistance to her energy. As she expanded her perception of the area, she eventually saw a large capsule that she could not peer into. She widened her focus to determine the size of it and to see if she could push through it.

Suddenly, she was thrown back like she had stepped onto a catapult!

# Chapter 18

It was an odd dream, but it kept calling him. He saw Merle dancing to a very strange drum beat. She danced like she was in a trance, but she was fully aware of herself. She pointed her finger at him, then curled it back, telling him to come to her.

Goose never hesitated when it came to his favorite mentor, but somehow, this did not feel right, so he turned over and continued his sleep.

In the morning, he immediately sought out Merle, or Mike. He felt he needed to look into what had happened. After searching the Matrix, he checked in with Beth to see if she knew of their whereabouts.

"I have not seen them in days. It feels like they do not live here anymore," she told him.

Goose then decided he would try to connect with them telepathically. He headed off to the forest to sit under a cedar tree. As he walked, he looked aside and noticed there were people in the wing that Merle had manifested. Instinctively, he headed to investigate.

When he opened the door, he was received by a person sitting in lotus position, floating in the air.

"Cool," he thought, so he immediately copied her. As they looked at each other, Lizu introduced herself and her fellow Pleiadeans.

"Your friend Merle has joined us in dealing with a serious situation. For her to succeed with this matter, she has ascended to a new level in her experience. She is now called Oona, the One. Tarita has also joined us, she is now known as Tan. Since you have been able to know us at this time, you are also to join us."

"Will the rest of my group be joining us, the Windsurfers?"

"Possibly, as the project unfolds, if their vibration is necessary to assist us, however, for now, it is just you."

At that, Goose settled back, accepting the situation, then glanced around the room. Oona was standing nearby, smiling at him, just waiting for him to recognize her. She came forward and joined them, giving Goose a big hug.

Lizu briefed Goose on the situation. Merle then suggested they visit the physical location as she and Tan had done most recently. Instantly, they were sitting in a forested park.

Goose looked around in dismay. "We have got to do something to fix this. This is not an ordinary problem for sure. Something has to be causing this. This is not just Mother Nature reacting to something we humans have created.

Goose immediately went into meditation so he could survey the situation. The drumming started. He could feel its pull, but he knew better. Instead, he listened inside the drumbeat, looking for its source. Soon, he could hear the churning of what sounded like a motor running, so he went inside that sound.

Whack! Goose found himself lying flat on the ground. "Holy smokes, that was powerful. It just threw me right out!"

He took a deep breath, shaking himself off. He looked at Oona, then proceeded to head right back in.

Whack! Right back where he had lain only a few minutes before.

"This is what we have been having trouble with, too. Every time we get to a certain level, whatever it is, throws us back out or tries to capture us. It just seems to know what we are trying to do and stops us in our tracks."

Goose thought about it for a minute, then suggested. "Maybe if we try getting close without using our human consciousness, it might not be able to detect that specific vibration."

With that, Tan appeared. "How about if I try to get closer in butterfly?"

Rachel then appeared as Tan transitioned herself. She tapped her wand above Tan causing her to glow brilliantly, and off she went.

Tan flew deep into the energy. It felt very strange, this energy oozing like a thick fluid, almost like molasses. It was very uncomfortable, but she was making progress. The consciousness of this mass did not seem to notice her.

Finally, she passed into a less dense energy. She hovered for a bit to look around and assess the new situation. There were the drummers! She had made it into the center. Now to find out what was the cause.

As she flitted around the area, she sensed a pull in one direction. It felt familiar, somewhat like the original pulling from the drumbeat. Cautiously, she approached, searching for the source.

Then, there it was! A huge orb. A gelatinous-looking blob that looked much like a garden slug! Yuk, was her only response! It looked awful!!! It just oozed negativity.

She watched it for a while to see if it would do anything or if it could move, but it just sat there. Then she tuned in on it energetically. If she thought looking at it was yukky, connecting to its energy was even worse!

The thing sucked energy into itself but expended none. It was like a big vacuum cleaner, except that it seemed to depend on negative energy for its sustenance. It just consumed negative energy in a never-ending cycle.

She paused for a moment to scan the area again, trying to find out where it would get its food from. Then she heard it... the crying... the crying of hunger and desperation!

She flitted off to see if she could find where the crying was coming from. Without emerging through the molasses-like membrane, Tan found herself in the school gymnasium. It was filled with the children that the people of the agency had collected.. many of them having passed away from starvation and trauma. This might be the doorway for the others to join her!

In seconds, she popped back into view, sitting between Oona and Goose. As she transitioned back into human, she raised her hand asking for a moment to recollect herself. This had been an exhausting expedition for Tan!

Finally, she was able to collect her thoughts well enough to tell what she had found out. Now, maybe they could make some headway!

Rachel and Lizu appeared so they could join in.

"Are you able to transform yourself, Goose?" Tan asked.

Shaking his head, laughing, he morphed into a beautiful dragonfly. Oona, not to be left out, thought it would be fun to be a dragonfly too, so she joined Goose. Soon, a beautiful butterfly and two dragonflies were off to solve this mystery!

Upon entering the gymnasium, the trio were greeted by the drumming. It did not concern them except to act as a guide to lead them back to the sluglike orb. Before they headed in that direction, though, the trio flew over the children, sending them loving energy. The children saw the butterfly and the dragonflies. They stopped crying so they could focus on the magic before them.

Oona swooped over the children, spraying them with a dusting the children soaked in through their skin that gave them food while Tan made it rain. Goose focused on their mindset, sending them calmness and a sense of well-being.

Once the children had settled down, they started to follow the drumbeat, but something had changed. The drumming was weaker. It made it harder to follow it, but they made their way slowly.

When they arrived at the orb, Tan immediately saw that it was much more negative than before. It was angry that the children had been tended to. They had tampered with its supply of negative energy!

---

Outside once again, they laughed with joy! Although this was not really a joyous occasion, they laughed because they now knew what had to be done to fix this situation!

They all danced through the air before returning to human form. Barrel rolls and deep dives were in order this day! Success was at hand!

"I think it is time for the Wind Surfers to help out," laughed Goose, and with that, they all appeared before them, musical instruments in hand!

"It's party time, gang! We need to make a lot of people happy here, so let's get playing!"

Forming a parade, all the Wind Surfers marched into town. They played the happiest music they could, marching right down the main street. At first, the locals just turned and stared. Some of them yelled profanities at them, but as we know about this special music, it soon captured their hearts.

People poured out of the buildings to follow the ensemble. They began singing with the music. Their anger and frustration melted away with each step. Finally, they reached the town square where they began dancing and laughing like they had not done for so long.

Of course, Goose pre-ordered a magical food truck! Free Mini Donuts for all! (made with lots of nutritious ingredients, of course!)

Once all the people in the town had danced themselves out and over-indulged on Mini Donuts, Oona took the microphone to address the people.

"We thank you for opening your hearts to us today. We have come to end this situation that has overcome you. We understand your pain. Our reason for being here is to help you heal and become whole again. Maybe even better than before."

"We have a task for you that is essential to the success of this mission. Even though it may be difficult for you, you must let yourself be happy and positive. We have discovered that there is an entity buried beneath your earth that feeds on negative energy. To bring its reign to an end, we must stop feeding it."

"Send no more of your children to that agency. It is part of the negative one's ploy to feed itself. When anyone from that agency approaches you, invite them to eat with you. We expect the orb will be very unhappy about our interference, but we are prepared to deal with it, and to bring this situation to a successful conclusion."

"I repeat, you must only do kind acts and have loving, generous thoughts, so this thing does not get fed anymore."

# Chapter 19

The locals had become so happy now they had danced to their heart's delight and filled up on Mini Donuts. They all pitched in, helping each other with the project. People hugged and hugged, moving joyously from person to person, sharing the positive energy.

In the meantime, Goose, Tan, and Oona headed back into the abyss. They knew they were in for some major resistance. Traveling back into the gymnasium, some very angry-looking guards immediately set them upon.

Oona, recalling the early days of solving crimes, magically projected positive golden energy at the guards. Instead of them becoming passive, they melted into blobs on the ground. Quickly realizing the guards were not human at all, but extensions of the blob, Oona set up an energy to draw all the guards out. As they appeared, they dropped to the ground until the entire area looked like a bunch of puddles, dark murky puddles.

With the guards now out of the way, Goose returned to human form momentarily to open the doors of the gymnasium. The children were now free! Their parents stood outside, ready to celebrate their return. There were a lot of smiling faces!

The drummers were really beating up a storm, literally, when the three re-entered the chasm. They did not look at the trio as they flew in, but they were ready for them. The music was almost unbearable... so fast and unbearably intense! Ordinary folks could not have survived!

Oona again sent the energy out to placate the drummers. At first, they did not respond, so Goose and Tan joined Oona in projecting the energy. The drummers played even faster. Their hands were almost invisible, they played so fast!

In the distance, they could see the creator of all this disturbance. It was angry. It was attempting to draw in more and more negative energy to keep itself fed. It knew its last line of defense was the drummers, so it poured all its energy into them. The drummers kept drumming... and growing larger and angrier with every beat.

"There must be another source of the negative energy! It is still being fed!" all three of them thought to each other.

---

Again, back to the outside world. They now had to find where another source of the negative energy could be coming from.

When they arrived back in the town, they could not believe their eyes. Police and other government officials were rounding up the locals in an attempt to prevent them from being positive and happy. They had separated all the children in an attempt to return them to the gymnasium.

The parents remembered their promise, though, and remained positive. They had just enough time to pass on the message to their children as well, so even though they were being mistreated, they kept smiling and resisting (in a positive way, of course).

Oona purposely taunted one of the government people so she could connect with their mind. As the agent approached, Oona projected gold light. It caused an opening in the woman's mind so she could gain access. Oona was shocked at what she learned.

The current leader of the government had seized complete control of the country, intending to enslave all the citizens. To complete this mission, she had commissioned a machine that would project negative energy into the atmosphere and the earth, causing catastrophic failure of any ecosystems in this region.

What she did not realize was that this orb was already resident in the underworld of this country. It had developed because of all the negative actions that had occurred in the area over so many, many years. Once the orb felt the machine taking hold, it seized the opportunity and magnified it until everything was in ruins.

The orb had become so powerful that it had seized the minds of the very leaders who had sought to take control, leaving them slaves themselves. There appeared to be no turning back now. Chaos was the path of this future, or so it thought!

There was a noisy shuffling behind Goose, then someone yelled at him, "What's this going off on an adventure without us?"

It was Condor! Or more correctly the whole of the Wind Surfers... with musical instruments!

"Boy, am I glad to see you guys. We really need to pull up the energy around here... quick!"

The Wind Surfers immediately formed another parade and marched back into the town. They played a beautiful, sweet melody that captured the hearts of the people, quickly bringing the chaos to an end. Even the government people and police officers were captivated!

All was well... at least at surface level.

"We need to find that machine," said Oona. "We need to figure out where it is. Who here can lead us to it, I wonder?"

She looked around at the government agents. She scanned each of their energy fields, trying to see if any of them knew anything that might help, but found nothing. Putting on her detective cap, she began looking for pieces to this undefined jigsaw puzzle.

"Of course!" she said to herself. "All of these people work for the same government agency, so all I need to do is climb the ladder. Eventually, I will find someone who knows where that machine is!"

Oona projected herself to the national head office of the agency. The negative air was so thick, it almost oozed. She ramped up her energy so she could keep herself clear as she surveyed the people in the office. She could feel she was in the right place, but not the perfect place.

She needed to get into someone's head, so picking a woman who sat alone in her office, she became her dragonfly again. That caught her attention!

The woman screamed and ran out of the room, yelling something about a monster flying at her! It was enough though, to let her get into the woman's mind.

The next step revealed itself quickly, and off she went, finding herself in a cave in a remote mountain. There was the machine. It seemed like a rather innocuous machine from this perspective, but she knew this was the main feed for the blob.

There was no one around, so Oona returned to human form, then proceeded to analyze the workings of the machine. She saw nothing she could dismantle to stop the machine. No panels or wires. It looked almost animal-like, self-sustaining.

Lizu then appeared beside Oona. "Let's combine our energies and visualize it disintegrating, Oona."

Rachel then appeared to join in as well, so the three of them focused together. The negative energy was so intense, they really had to work to get their energy high enough to overcome it, however, as we know, good always wins over bad!

Soon the machine began to falter. At first, the hum missed a few beats, then there were visible signs of the machine's termination. Pieces of the machine began melting and falling to the floor... then silence.

Before long, the machine was just a gigantic pile of melted jelly on the floor of the cave! The negative energy it had emitted had stopped.

As the trio stepped out of the cave, they realized they were not on earth. The machine had been projecting the energy from an asteroid far in space.

It was a good thing, because very quickly, there were the beginnings of an earthquake.

"Let's get out of here and back to the town!" Rachel yelled. And with that, they were gone... and in seconds, so was the asteroid as it exploded into billions of little pieces.

# Chapter 20

The sun was shining as Oona, Lizu, and Rachel arrived back at the little town. The first thing they noticed was green! Lots of green! The earth was coming back to life!

A little Robert's Geranium poked its nose out of the ground, so Oona reached down and stroked its leaves, causing the entire area to be filled with this beautiful plant. The scent of geranium filled the air, lifting the spirits of the trio to a new high. They felt so connected!

In the distance, they could hear the Wind Surfers playing a raucous tune. One could say some jigs were being pounded into the earth on this day! However, there was still work to be done on this site.

Rachel suggested they take a few moments to meditate so they could be sure of the next steps. They needed to make sure they extinguished this event so there would be no repeats.

Heading back into the cave, the first thing they noticed was the quiet. No more drummers, in fact, not only the music had ceased, but the drummers had vaporized, leaving not a trace. The blob had shrunk to a tiny drop compared to its original size, but still showed signs of life. It was not the threatening orb it had once been, though.

During their meditations, they received the message that the orb was not to be extinguished, as it still served a purpose. It was to be allowed to survive, but only in a very minuscule form. To ensure its imprisonment, the trio reshaped the capsule it had created for itself as protection, with no capacity for escape.

The last step was the closing of the cave. With one swish of Rachel's hand, the enormous cave became a sealed pile of rubble.

On that note, the land returned to its former beauty. The crops glistened in the summer sun; fruit popped out like popping popcorn as the fruit trees rejoiced in their return to life.

---

The scent of rich lavender filled the nostrils of all the people as Rachel appeared over the cheerful crowds, still dancing, like they had never danced before.

*"I am Rachel. I serve the Universal God that created this earth and all that exists. I invite you to join me in this moment of knowing yourself through the eyes of God."*

The crowd halted on the spot, looking up into the sky. They could not believe their eyes. A beautiful lady with long blond hair wearing a lavender gown was floating in the air just above them.

There had been so many unusual and exciting events in recent days, though, that not one person thought it out of the ordinary that an angel spoke to them now. They all remained quiet, waiting.

*"We are blessed with peace and joy on this day as our children are returned to our lives. Allow the love for each other to flow freely, not just for now, but at all times.*

*Let us never forget the memories of this event. The feelings and memories shall always remain in the subtle corners of our minds. You will always know what it has been like to reside in the energies of fear. It is your own fears and negative thinking that has brought this situation to life... and it can return if enough people choose to express this energy through choices of selfishness, greed, or lack of caring about your people and your planet.*

*It is your choice, now and always, to live in harmony with the Universe God. It is your choice to empower each other through acts of healthy kindness that will support your growth as a soul. We are all aspects of our beloved God. We live in our purpose by helping ourselves by helping others to be the perfect expression of Universal Love.*

*Should you choose to express your lives in the highest expression you have inside you, you will find your life will prosper in ways you never imagined. God gave you free dominion to express yourself in your unique truth and to support others in the same.*

*You have embraced the positive force today. Let it form the basis of how life is to be, not just for today, but for all days, forever. Through this choice, all will be healed.*

*I am Rachel, I stand by you and for you, in the name of our Universal God."*

As Rachel faded away, a dusting of gold powder floated down from the sky. As the townfolk breathed in it, they each kneeled down and sobbed, not in sadness, but in joy. In this moment, they each came to know themselves.

---

It seemed like the celebrating would never end. Nobody wanted it to, that was for sure. The Wind Surfers never ran out of songs to play, so all the townspeople kept dancing... and eating Mini Donuts!

It did not take long for them to begin chatting with each other, even though their feet still moved to the songs. They wondered what would happen in their lives now that this huge negative energy had been vanquished. They had listened to Rachel, now they wanted to know what they could do. Maintaining a positive outlook on life was easy if everyone could keep listening to the music and dancing. However, there was a lot of work to be done to pick up the pieces of their ruined lives. And what about the families of the children who had perished? How could they move forward in their lives and find happiness?

# Chapter 21

Rose sat at her desk working on papers as she waited for her guest. "He should be along any minute, so I think I will wrap this up for now," she thought to herself, and in that exact moment, there was a knock at her door.

"I am Reverend Harry," he said as Rose invited him in. "I am so glad you have time to meet with me. I really need someone to chat with... in confidence."

"Sit down where you like, Reverend Harry. Would you like a cup of tea?"

As Rose poured her special tea, Reverend Harry got settled in. Saying nothing for the moment, it was easy to see there was something serious on his mind.

"I have been having the same dream over and over each night for weeks now. I do not make it a habit of consorting with Tarot Readers, but the dream told me to reach out to you. I guess the only way to get this dream to stop is to see why we need to meet.

I am a good Christian minister. I have led my flock faithfully for over fifteen years. I do not know why it has come about that I must have a Tarot Card reading. It is completely contradictory to my faith."

Reverend Harry sat nervously as he spoke, actually wishing he could just bolt for the door, however, he knew he would never find peace if he did that, so he sat.

"My, this tea is delicious," he said. "Is it a special blend?"

Giggling quietly, Rose nodded, waiting for him to continue, but he sat quietly as he passed into a meditative state. Then he heard a voice from the sky:

*"I am Rachel. I serve the Universal God that created this earth and all that exists. I invite you to join me in this moment of knowing yourself through the eyes of God."*

Rachel was silent for a moment, then she let herself appear before Reverend Harry. She spoke kindly, but directly, to him.

*"Reverend Harry, you have served your people well for these many years. You have been invited here today because of your service. As you will soon come to know, your teachings and offerings to your flock will be expanded, as the need is very great at this time. As you know, there has been much unrest in your town and in your congregation in recent years. Now that the perpetrator has been brought to rest, we invite you to join us in raising the level of consciousness of your fellow citizens.*

*Although the teachings you have provided for these many years have served the purpose of making believers of your flock, it is now time for you to be of service in helping each of them to raise their consciousness to a new level of spirituality, higher than even you have experienced through your meditations."*

As Reverend Harry listened, he impulsively sipped his tea. He thought he was hallucinating when he saw a man before him that looked like he could be his son. The young man smiled at him, then pointed back to the way Reverend Harry had been coming from. Turning, he immediately realized he was looking back at his future. In some way, it seemed odd, and yet rather normal, to be looking at his future as if it were the past.

Reverend Harry knew. It indeed was time for him to change his role. He knew that his flock no longer needed a guide or an interpreter. They needed a leader, a leader that could show them the true path to freedom through acceptance of Universal Consciousness.

*"We wish for you, if you accept your new role, to allow your church and school to become the launching pad for spiritual growth in your community and the surrounding areas. So many families need and want spiritual guidance because of these recent events. Do you accept, Reverend Harry? This will not be an easy task for you unless you are willing to be open to our guidance, a guidance that will support you in becoming all that you have the capacity to be."*

Reverend Harry just smiled in acceptance. His dream was finally coming true.

*"My dearest Rose will help you set up the new center. She has much experience in this matter. Under her guidance, you will find the new life you so desire, but you must be open to a new, more expanded understanding of your world. If you find that the change is too much for you, you must remove yourself from this project. We believe that the love you carry in your heart will help you in mastering the new consciousness that awaits you."*

In only seconds, Reverend Harry found himself alone with Rose. He awaited the beginning of his new life. Gone was the desire to bolt!

Rose smiled at him as she saw the acceptance merge into his consciousness. All Rose said was, "Let us begin!"

---

Reverend Harry stepped up to the microphone. He was used to speaking at his church, but this was completely new for him. He felt very nervous as he looked over the hundreds of people still in the park.

The Wind Surfers had stopped playing dance music, but chanted quietly while he prepared to introduce the next chapter in the lives of his flock. With no introduction, the crowd became silent.

"Our fair town has been reborn. It is a time of new beginnings. I have accepted the task of forming a center for spiritual learning from our church to provide the opportunity for every person here, no matter their belief, so they may come to know, integrate and express their true purpose."

The faces of each of the Wind Surfers broke into gigantic smiles as Reverend Harry introduced Rose. She looked at them and bowed, proudly smiling in recognition.

"Along with my new associate, Rose, we will provide programs for individual adults, children, and families that will support each of you in every way to integrate and maintain new levels of knowing yourselves. Even I am on the learning curve with this new project. I will no longer act as your guide or your support person. I will lead all of you through my own actions, allowing myself to be freed from the limitations I believed were the only truth. I state here today in front of each of you as my witnesses, that a new level of spiritual consciousness is now germinating in our lives that will leave the old truths as dust. I solemnly vow to lead you in your own journey as I evolve in mine, in the name of the true Universal God."

The townspeople had always loved their Reverend Harry, so they cheered and cheered when he had finished his speech. He then turned toward Rose and invited her to speak. As she stepped up, the Wind Surfers played an enchanting flute melody that caused everyone in the audience to hold hands together as one body swaying to the rhythm of the tune.

"It is a time for love, a time for unity with all. We have lived as separated beings for long enough. It is time to set aside petty differences, dysfunctional living and to live in the grace that we were born into.

Out of tragedy, learning is born. That learning leads us to a higher knowing, that leads us to the ultimate desire of all beings... love. We begin today a new life that only supports being in the healthiest form possible on any level. Through our Beloved Rachel, we have transcended the old life we all have grown tired from. We begin today to live in the good graces of The Universal God. This new life, a life of true happiness and freedom that lets our own energy breathe freely throughout the universe, has energized us.

The only contribution each of you needs to make to embrace this new life is the willingness to be open to learn and accept a new way to live. The new center that will open soon will be your doorway to the new life. Reverend Harry, Guardian Angel Rachel, and I invite you to join in and become!"

Rose looked to the side at the Wind Surfers. The party roared into action once more.

---

It didn't take long for the church and school to be converted into the new training center, especially since there was no need for a residence. Reverend Harry was a little unnerved, though, that by the time the partying was over, so were the renovations.

"I do not understand," Reverend Harry stammered. "How could the entire property be renovated, almost in a blink of an eye, Rose?

These changes should have taken weeks to do. Was there some kind of magic involved in this? I get nervous when things happen that I cannot explain to myself. Please help me, Rose. I am trying."

"Jesus was a carpenter, was he not? Likely a pretty good one too! It is important that you just trust the higher powers that are working with us, Reverend Harry. We need to get the new program working quickly, so the time to do manual labor would be too costly in the time we need to help these people.

Go look about the center, feel all the changes, and tell me if they feel worthy of being nervous about. This is all part of the new consciousness. The only difference between what occurred here and what would have been done in the past is time. We have just used a shorter time frame. You will get used to it once you see it happening in other ways as we carry on.

Our egos are used to life being at a recognizable pace, and it rebels when the norm changes. Can you imagine how our great grandparents would feel with so many of the things we take for granted now? Just using a telephone might be too much for them!"

Harry smiled a nervous smile but relaxed, soon letting himself enjoy the new facilities.

"When do we have our first students, Rose?"

"Your timing is impeccable sir!" At that Rose turned to invite several families into the center.

Reverend Harry invited the guests into the first large room he saw available. There were no chairs in the room, but there were piles of gym mats. He groaned as he wondered what he had gotten himself into.

"We heard there was going to be an introductory yoga class here today, so we are all here to try it. Even our kids want to try it. This is so nice having a place where we can bring the whole gang and share something meaningful," offered a parent as they walked in.

The room was filled to capacity as Teesha walked in. Rose smiled and gave her a big welcoming hug. The new center was now alive!

# Chapter 22

**"** *Being able to separate the workings of the ego from truth is the first goal of true spirituality,"* Rachel whispered softly as the crowd meditated.

*"We have to learn to differentiate between the voices that speak in our minds. Too often we run amuck when the information propounded by an egoic voice is treated as Spirit working inside us.*

*Learning to feel Spirit is the key to knowing. So much of what we believe to be true is actually false. Just because we have learned to believe it as truth, does not make it so.*

*Being conscious of what you think, learning to discern what you believe is true from what is actually true, will provide you with so much new freedom... and true personal power."*

Teesha smiled and stretched as she opened her eyes to meet the loving looks of her students. The class had gathered for several months now, not one person had dropped out or even missed a class. Even Reverend Harry had become an avid participant.

After the class had finished, Reverend Harry spoke with Teesha. "I would never have believed even a few months ago that I would be meditating and practicing yoga, my friend. I must say I do a pretty mean Downward Dog, eh!"

Teesha laughed and gave him a big hug. "Your Cobra is really outstanding as well! How are you doing with the lessons that Rachel provides during the meditation though, Reverend Harry?"

"To be honest, I find it so challenging to leave behind all that I have based my life upon for so many years. That ego is a sneaky fella!

It seems to be so much easier to live now that I can just turn in for a few minutes, take a few deep breaths, and voila, I can make a clear choice... and even if I make the wrong choice, I do not beat myself up for it. I just see the error for what it is and make a new choice."

"Yes," agreed Teesha. "I know for myself that it took quite a long time to learn to be in my body so I could listen to its communications instead of living my life based on what my ego saw as the right answer.

Moving past guilt, jealousy, greed, being needy... all those things that impeded my life force have been so freeing.

Being of the Indian culture, it has been quite interesting to learn about the various modes of Christianity as an outsider. Did you know that Jesus the Christ trained in India for a while as part of his initiation? He surely understood the dangers of a runaway ego!

This modern world has sure let the ego take over, to the point where Spirit has a really difficult time being heard at all. However, spirit always works around what the human mind can concoct... sometimes providing huge lessons that could have been omitted had people been able to hear."

"What do you mean, Teesha? Aren't some things beyond human understanding and they just happen?"

"That again is why we are here now, so people can learn to separate egoic choices from supportive purposeful choices. When Spirit is stifled, the energy becomes congested. This does not matter if it is for one person or for the entire world. If a choice is made and held inside that is contrary to truth, it will eventually express.

World Wars are an example of egoic beliefs being placed in front of truths. Do you think that the wars would have occurred if people had been thinking beyond the ego? People bought into the belief that the other side was bad, so they had to fight back. What if the governments declared war, and nobody showed up to fight?

The same is true of the personal wars we fight inside of ourselves. We learn as children that we are not worthy of love through our family environment, then as adults, we try to fit into the world and build relationships. The result being divorces and illness, just because we have not learned how to see when we are living in ego. Our spirit energy wants to express but cannot because we have been trained to only trust what the ego tells us. That energy becomes congested inside us and eventually forces its way out through disease."

"Isn't that the purpose of the church to help people let go and alleviate their pain and suffering?" asked Reverend Harry.

"This was the original intention, however, the ego got in control of the churches as well. The church leaders believed the masses needed to be controlled, so introducing the need to suffer and feel guilty for being a sinner overrode the original intention to help people become in tune with the spirit inside them.

As you have realized yourself in the last few months, some churches often purposely mesmerized people into believing that they are limited beings that hold no personal power. In many cases, making it so that people did not even have the privilege of making their own decisions. Having one's thoughts or beliefs restricted because they might not support the current belief of the clergy of their church is so debilitating. After all, how can any religion help a person become closer to its God if it is based on shrouding the truth?"

# Chapter 23

Reverend Harry prayed earnestly as he prepared to retire to sleep. He still felt uncertain about his volunteering to "change" religions, so as he prayed he asked for a sign to confirm which path was for him.

Reverend Harry fell into a deep sleep. It was not long before Rachel came to visit with him... and she brought a friend.

"My dear Harry, you have suffered so with this change in your life. We know it is so hard for you to let go of what you thought was the truth for so much of your life. In fact, for you, it was the truth, but it was the truth of a less enlightened mind.

Today, it gives me great pleasure to invite you to meet a person you have believed in for so many years. The opportunity is now upon you to learn from the Master himself."

As she spoke, she invited her friend to step forward. Harry recognized him immediately. Even in his sleep, he trembled in awe.

"There is a hierarchy amongst the guides and angels that exist to support mankind in finding themselves. Only God receives higher recognition than a Master. I introduce you to Master Jesus."

As Master Jesus smiled at Harry, he began to cry, in relief.

"I thought I had rejected you by accepting this new understanding, Master Jesus. I love you beyond all else."

And Master Jesus replied, "Harry, you could not reject me, for I am. To reject me would be to reject all. You are now embarking on a new learning, one that will bring you not only closer to me, but closer to being like me.

"Master Jesus, would you mind if I asked you a question that has really been bothering me?'"

"Please, my friend."

"It is said that one day you will return to earth to lead us again. When will that be?"

Jesus was taken aback for one second, then smiled at Reverend Harry.

"This is a common misconception. I am glad to put you straight and ease your mind. I am not coming back."

At that, Reverend Harry froze, not believing his ears.

"Harry, in order for me to return, I would have to have left. So... I will not return... because I never left.

When I passed through the Great Transition, the vibration of my physical body rose to a level equal to that of my soul so I could return to the vibration I now work through. This allows me to periodically re-manifest in the physical in whatever form I choose. That is why you can see me right now. I manifest in the form you can accept. We are quite accommodating!

It was once said- I am the Way, The Light, and the Life. This always has been the truth; however, you will now know that my role is and has always been that of the teacher. In this new, higher consciousness, you will now integrate and grow into what we call Christ Consciousness. As you learn and experience new levels of consciousness, you will experience the skills to be a Master. It is our desire now that all humans evolve as Masters. It is our desire, Harry, that you work with us to help your people evolve. Now, enough of this serious talk! Let's have some fun!"

And with that Rachel, Master Jesus, and Reverend Harry immediately transformed into Golden Butterflies!

As they flitted about laughing and doing all kinds of acrobatics, they were joined by hundreds of other Golden butterflies!

The last thing Harry heard as he let the dream go was, "We are all family, Harry!"

---

When morning came, Harry laid in his bed smiling at the world, his new world. He could hardly wait for his parishioners.

"No, wait," he realized. "I do not have parishioners anymore. They are my family!" And with that, he turned over and wept like he had not never cried before. Harry finally felt like he belonged.

It was a good thing the first class was not beginning until late morning, so Harry had time to get himself together. When he finally arrived at the center, he was ready!

Everyone really noticed the difference in Harry this day. When they greeted him as Reverend Harry, he informed them that he no longer was a minister, so they could just call him by his name. However, most of them protested and said they would call him Reverend Harry, anyway!

Harry laughed and gave every person a great big hug. Then it was on to yoga!

As the class was wrapping up, Teesha called to Harry, "I understand you had a very special dream last night, Harry. Would you like to share it with the class?"

Harry smiled proudly and said, "Guardian Angel Rachel came to me last night in my sleep. She introduced me to... Master Jesus! They are good friends up in the Angel world! Master Jesus told me that my job is to help myself and others to be like him. We need to work together to learn to master life so we can be like him... and then we became butterflies just so we could have some fun together! We all flitted about and did acrobatics. Then a whole bunch more butterflies joined us. It was really fun!"

Harry felt so emotional about telling about his dream that he burst into tears again. Many of his family came to hug him.

---

Harry soon started to see a visible difference in his life. He became more relaxed. He realized the ongoing war in his mind was fading away. His internal demand to be perfect became a distant memory. He finally came to accept himself, perfect or not!

The new Harry found a zest in his step as this new freedom relaxed his body. He became a pretty amazing yoga guy! (That is what he calls himself!) He could bend in ways he never could before, just because he was more relaxed in his mind. As the limitations dissolved away in Harry's life, his personal power soared.

By the flash of an Angel's wand, Harry had skills he never would have believed... or accepted in his prior life. He became a powerful healing facilitator and medium. He could draw the right answers almost any time... right from the clouds, so to say!

Harry first realized his new healing skill when a man came into the center. He looked very pale and walked slowly, dragging his leg. He reached out to Harry just in time to stop himself from falling face-first onto the floor. When Harry grabbed him to stop his fall, the man began convulsing mildly. Within a minute, he stood up and walked away as any normal, healthy person would.

He did not even realize the change because his consciousness had changed as well! Harry certainly noticed. He stared at his hands. They were tingling so much, they almost hurt.

A while later, a woman came running into the center looking for Harry. When she found him, she gave him the biggest hug Harry had ever known. "Thank you so much, Harry, for giving me my husband back! He had a stroke after our child died because he felt there was no point in living. He is as good as new now!"

The people who called him Reverend Harry continued to do so out of love for him. In fact, they loved the new Harry more than they could have imagined. He became a shining example of a fully empowered human being.

The aura of the town changed too. The struggles of people lost; people whose only purpose had been to survive above all else transitioned into one large family of people who supported each other and made life not only tolerable but a delightful place to be.

Neighborhood barbecues became standard fare on weekends, except interestingly there was a drastic increase of portobello mushroom burgers instead of the typical beef burger! Harry and Rose had a really challenging time keeping up with all the invitations.

Even the nature around town changed! The trees grew full and tall, especially the cedar trees that smiled proudly in the sun. Flowers poked out everywhere, coloring up the landscape. Out on the farms, the farmers planted crops that supported the biodiversity of the region. In return, the crops yielded more than the farmers could ever imagine... and to pass on the abundance; the farmers gave back more to the earth by learning to farm with nature instead of despite nature.

There were no longer any poor people in the area. Those who had formerly struggled, realized that their poverty had only been an illusion they acted out. As they came to a higher level of self-realization, they became more engaged in participating in helping to develop a healthy economy. They knew they no longer wanted handouts because handouts diminished their own personal integrity.

The local economy exploded as the little farm community grew into a modern training center. Local businesses became more successful as people from farther away came to experience what the townsfolks enjoyed in their new lives.

The new center had achieved its goal... and the only way from here was up!

As a special bonus to the townsfolk... within months, all the families who had lost a child were pregnant! Life is so grand!

Harry was a very contented man as he watched his people come to the center to take part in the various classes, but he really smiled when the baby bumps began to show!

# Chapter 24

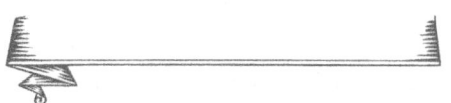

Deep inside my bark, I feel love for all,
    I reach to the sky and spread my bows wide to thank my God,
    My roots reach into the earth to feed me and give me strength.
    How could I feel anything but joy with all that I am blessed?
    I love that I am a cedar tree, the holiest of trees, that is love.
    I reach out to all I can and invite you inside me.
    When you share your love with me I can reach so high into the sky
    I can bring the stars down to play.
    I share my love with you, so you can be everything, all at one time.
    Come sit inside me and feel the wind rocking gently and feel the warm bask of the sun.
    There is nothing on earth greater than the joy of having you in me.
    We share all that is created by our God and gratefully return the love.

---

Goose woke up and stretched his arms out quickly realizing he was now inside the cedar tree instead of leaning against it as he often did. It felt very cozy. He felt loved.

He had heard what the cedar tree had said. He knew cedar trees were very wise and holy. He felt so very fortunate to be in this state of love. He knew it was his mission to bring other people to share what the cedar tree offered.

Goose stayed inside his tree for a very long time. He focused on sending love to all the people that had brought him to this point. He missed Mike and Tomas so very much, but he knew they had gone to be with the Pleiadeans. He also knew that if they were needed, they could be here in an instant. Deep down inside, he hoped that would never need be.

Suddenly, a little twitch made his cheek tingle. In front of him flitting her wings was his little friend Papi. She looked anxious, trying to get him to follow her. It was time to get himself back to the outer world.

As he stepped out of the tree, he stopped for a moment to pat his friend and to give thanks before following Papi back into the Matrix.

"You are just in time, Goose, now we can begin our meeting," Condor said as he led the group into a meditation of thanks before getting down to the real purpose of this get-together.

"It seems we have a new project to begin working on. Finally, we can work on helping Mother Earth. There is an enormous boom of plastic garbage floating out in the middle of the ocean. It is believed that it has caught hundreds of sea life in it. This boom is so large and dirty that it actually is impacting the ph. balance of the ocean in that area.

We need to figure out how to fix this situation and get it done, once and for all. If this problem gets any worse, it will start affecting weather patterns and possibly cause some geological activity. After all, Mother Nature will only tolerate so much before she uses whatever method she needs to fix the problem."

---

They thought they would be at a disadvantage having to work on this project on their own, but each of the Wind Surfers knew inside that this was their time to shine. After all, they were grownups now too. (Even Papi!)

Little did they know they had a cheering squad far away in the heavens watching them! Oona, Tan, Rachel, and Lizu all watched from their home in The Pleiades as each of the Wind Surfers discussed this new project.

---

"Let's fly out there and have a look. Then we can get a better idea of what the situation is," suggested Raven. At that, they all closed their eyes, and off they went.

As they arrived above the scene, every one of them began to cry... the sheer dimensions of the problem were so overwhelming, it just got to them. Being so connected to the vibrations of Mother Earth, they could feel the pain being caused by the problem.

They let themselves cry for a while, then, even though they still felt overwhelmingly sad, they surveyed the situation.

Even from their vantage point, high in the sky, they could not see the ends of this mass. They could see the massive damage it was causing. The water in the area had turned yellow from the change in the Ph of the water. It was so acidic that only a lazy jellyfish swam by. It felt like the water was choking from lack of oxygen.

"If people only understood how a plastic wrapper or a plastic bottle mindlessly tossed on the ground hundreds of miles away from here can add to this problem. The wind picks up the tossed garbage in an attempt to clean up the planet in that area. Then it gets dumped into a stream which ends up in a river and eventually finds its way to the ocean.

This area is the belly button of our planet. Everything ends up here... and there is a lot of everything right here. Now we have to figure out what to do," Goose cried as he sent his thoughts out to all the people on the planet, pleading for them to understand.

"Let's have a look underneath," Goose suggested to the others. They each reformed themselves into a sea animal, so they would feel more comfortable under the mass. Goose became a bottle-nosed dolphin and dove from high above, straight into the water.

As fast as they hit the water, they were back out; the water so lacking in oxygen, they gasped for air. Their underwater exploration ended quickly, however; they did get a chance to make a brief survey of some of the underside, so they had a better idea of what the situation presented.

Condor offered, "I think we need to grind the mass so we can separate the water from it and break it up to create some space for the air to get through. Most of this stuff is just gooey, It has broken down from the acidity of the water, but it has nowhere to go, so it is just lying like a big whitish duvet on a massive bed."

You gotta love these guys! As fast as Condor spoke, Raven appeared, driving a huge three-wheeler tractor with giant balloon tires. It even had a special device under the belly that reached down into the mass to pull the gucky stuff right up into the belly of the machine.

Almost as quickly, everyone had their machine (even Papi) busy chewing up the mess!

These machines had a very special technique that chewed the mass up into microscopic bites... but that was only the beginning. If the residue was spat back out into the ocean in its current state, it was minute enough that when fish returned to the area, they would likely digest it.

No, this was not the conclusive answer.

Once the residue was ground to its smallest particulate, it went through a final processor where it was returned to its original form... carbon.

As they released the carbon, it fell back into the water and eventually sank down to the bottom of the ocean.

The Wind Surfers worked tirelessly for days, taking breaks only to sleep and refresh themselves. They were going to clean this mess up once and for all before it was too late!

After they had worked on cleaning it up for several more days, they noticed that the size of the problem was not getting proportionately smaller.

Goose shook his head and said to the others, "The garbage is collecting faster than we can transition it. I can't believe how dirty and thoughtless people can be! We need to rev this up so we can get ahead of it!"

Instantly, Rachel appeared, swooshing her magic wand over the area. Each of the machines became ten times as big. The big balloon tires alone stood twenty feet high.

She smiled and waved at her beloved children, then said, "*This has to be done as close to the physical realm as possible to truly clean things up. Good work, my children!*"

The machines roared as they chomped away at blazing speed. Now they were finally making headway!

As the carbon floated down into the ocean below, it accumulated on the floor. Once their work had reached a tipping point, the ocean water began to return to its natural color. The carbon was absorbing the acidity, causing the water to return to a more alkaline state.

As the carbon built up and broke down into very fine particulate, it formed a layer of soil, for miles, and miles in every direction! This was so great!

Plants began to spring up on the ocean floor! It was only going to be a matter of time before fish would return and the ecosystem could stabilize. There were gigantic smiles, albeit exhausted ones, on the faces of each of the workers.

As a reward to themselves, the gang decided it was time for a little fun. Back into the water again!

Eight dolphins soon were having the time of their lives, basking in the sun, really enjoying the nice clean water. Hummingbird, of course, was doing flips and belly flops, splashing all his friends, being the over-energetic guy everybody knew and loved.

They were having so much fun they did not notice they had attracted some guests. There were now not just eight dolphins kibitzing in the water, but eighty! The entire area became like a three-ring circus. Some were surfing on the high waves, some were crashing on their backs, then springing right back up into the air only to dive deep into the crystal clear water. Everybody was having the time of their life!

Finally, one of the newcomer dolphins spoke to the Wind Surfers "Thank you for reducing this problem. We could not come to this area that we love for a very long time. We hope you can erase this problem, so it does not come back again."

At that, all the newcomer dolphins rose out of the water, bowed to their new friends, and did a reverse tail dance away in appreciation.

"Let's get this mess finished, so any sea life that wants to enjoy this space can come here safely and prosper. Let's get our engines started!" Goose cheered his friends on.

Having made friends with the dolphins made each of the Wind Surfers even more determined to eliminate the garbage completely, so the ocean could completely return to its former splendor.

By the end of one very busy month, the project was complete-ish. The tides still brought more garbage, but it was not causing serious harm... for the moment.

Condor re-invented his machine so that it automatically captured any new garbage that appeared... and!!!! It ran on its own. Since it was made from the ethers, it never needed maintenance and did not use any fuel. It could just chug away on its own, keeping the ocean clean!

Back home at the Matrix, there were some very tired folks. They had worked tirelessly, and now it was time to rest. Into the forest, they stumbled in search of their favorite cedar tree. Soon, quiet, deep breathing was all that was heard from inside the trees.

When they were finally feeling rested enough to take part in life again, they met in the yoga room. The combination of resting inside their cedar tree, playing with the dolphins, and having seen the damage created by thoughtless human beings, then working diligently to fix the problem, left each of them feeling quite perplexed.

They knew the mass of plastic would likely form again, as the amount of pollution collected would become too much for Condor's machine, but they had no idea how to truly stop the cause. They all felt melancholy as they asked in their minds the same questions over and over.

Finally, a brilliant light shone above them as Rachel appeared.

*"We all know this has been very challenging for each of you. We know that the concept that created and maintains the existence of this problem is beyond your understanding.*

*Human beings, the world over, need to raise their consciousness to understand how important it is to look after Mother Earth. All the conventions by world leaders mean nothing if just one person discards a plastic wrapper carelessly.*

*It is our ambition that humans can ascend to a level where they can understand that their participation and membership in nature is paramount to the best health of this planet.*

*Humans are the only animals on this planet that hold the leash on nature. If humans choose to continue to act carelessly with their refuse, then Mother Earth becomes ill. If humans embrace the energies of Mother Nature and strive to become one with her, then all can be great.*

*It is the attitude of human beings that causes the great changes in weather systems; the increased pressure of hurricanes, more earthquakes, dramatic weather shifts; all caused by uncaring humans.*

*All that is needed to change, is a little sensitivity. Tousle a dandelion's head instead of picking it!*

*Enjoy the flavor of that apple they eat. Appreciate nature in its simplest beauty... and all will be well!*

*Humans need to understand that working with sustainability needs to have a holistic approach. Driving in their big fuel-guzzling cars to rallies so they can protest oil pipelines is no better than gorging on bags of potato chips while trying to lose weight.*

*Sustainability starts with the first breath in the morning. Eat and enjoy good food, minimize garbage and process it properly, get plenty of exercise, do your best in everything and give gratitude to everything in your life... that is the start of sustainability and caring for your planet."*

# Chapter 25

Reverend Harry was sitting in lotus position meditating when the Wind Surfers descended on him. Well, they didn't really descend on him, they came in quietly, and seeing him smiling away as he meditated, they all joined him on the floor.

They thought about having him join him in a counsel room in the clouds, but they thought that might be a little too much for him, so they waited for him to open his eyes. Their meeting would have to be in the yoga room.

When he finally opened his eyes, the first thing he saw was eight sets of eyes, showering him with love. Reverend Harry had learned to be open and accepting... he knew today was going to be the beginning of something special!

"You are the musicians!" Harry laughed. "This is a special treat. What brings you here today, my friends? Do you want tea?"

Instantly, each of the Wind Surfers conjured a big cup of steamy tea for themselves... and one for Harry. Harry shook his head, then laughed nervously. His tea was absolutely perfect. Just the right amount of honey and cream. He wondered where the limit was with these people!

"Reverend Harry, we would like to work with you on a special project, if you are willing," started Condor.

"We need someone who can relate directly to people to make the highest impact," said Raven.

Unable to contain himself any longer, Hummingbird began bouncing and flitting up into the air, making quite a spectacle of himself. He was just so excited about this project and helping his friend, Mother Nature.

"I do not know what this special project is yet, but I am in," Reverend Harry quickly stated. "I love the enthusiasm... and I recall very well the important contribution you people made to saving our town. What are we going to do?"

Goose told him about the work they had just completed. He then told him about how they all felt so sad because, even though they had cleaned up the mess, they had not resolved the problem. Creating a satisfactory resolution to the problem was the next project.

"Cool," laughed Harry. "I would never in a day, a few years ago have dreamed that I, a simple small-town minister, could transition into this fine soul worker I embrace today, and now to become an environmentalist as well!!! Let's get at it! What do I need to do?"

It was Papi's turn to jump in. She had been quiet for much too long, so she spoke as loud as her tiny little voice could muster and laid out the group's plan.

---

The meeting room was filled with local residents. They were excited to be hearing Reverend Harry speak today. All they knew was that he had news about an extensive project that needed their help. They were absolutely there for him, whatever he wanted.

When he stepped up to the microphone, the entire crowd jumped up and started cheering and clapping. Harry could never get used to so much approval. He just blushed and waited for them to calm down.

"My friends", he started. "We have a project that is so big and so important that we can no longer wait to get it mobilized. It involves every one of us, and in fact, every person on this planet. Despite its size, it is simple to take part. We just have to be mindful and do it.

You probably recognize these fine folks standing behind me. They call themselves the Wind Surfers. You likely remember them as the musicians that played that special music for us when we most needed it so long ago!"

And with that, the crowd was up again. The cheering and hooting went on almost forever. Hummingbird did his best to behave himself but finally began bouncing up in the air. Raven and Condor, standing beside him, held him down. After all, these fine folks were not quite ready for everything yet!

Reverend Harry told the crowd, once it had settled down again, about the project the gang had just returned from. He then chatted about how massive the oozing mass of garbage had become.

"We have developed some workshops for you to participate in so we can begin producing new products from the waste plastics instead of just collecting them, then shipping them off to another country so it becomes their problem. We are going to make an industry of this problem.

However, we intend this project to be temporary. Why?

Because we need to re-think plastics. At the end of the day, even when we repurpose the plastic. Eventually, it will need to be either repurposed again or it will end up as garbage. So, for now, we will re-engineer it into useful things we can use in our lives, hopefully replacing products that require being taken from nature.

The more important job is to find ways to reduce the amount of unnecessary plastic waste we create, to eventually eliminate this product altogether.

The third aspect of the project, and the most important one, is to change our minds and the actions that caused this to become a problem in the first place. After all, it is not the plastic that is the problem, it is the attitude of humans about how they treat our beloved planet that is the problem.

If a person truly, truly cares about themselves, then they also care about their environment; their families, their neighbors, and their planet. Didn't someone once say- Cleanliness is next to godliness?

Out of sight, out of mind has been the prevalent attitude since mankind came into being. If we don't change our attitude in this matter quickly, this adage will be in reference to humans themselves. We will pollute ourselves right off this planet!

We need to clean up our attitudes and our relationship with Mother Earth, and it has to start with the way we think about our place on this planet."

Again, the crowd burst into a loving roar that went on and on. Everyone was so enthusiastic that the Wind Surfers spontaneously broke out in song (even though they had not brought their instruments (wink, wink)).

And Hummingbird! Well, the boys could not hold him any further. Unbridled enthusiasm cannot be contained!

So the meeting melted into a party. People danced and partied. Hummingbird bounced relentlessly and Papi got into it too! Nobody thought twice about the cool butterfly doing aerobatics over their heads!

---

A new industry was born in the town. It all seemed so easy that many wondered why this did not happen sooner. The conclusion was- awareness! If one does not know there is a problem, one does not look for a solution!

However, just because one is not aware of the problem, it does not mean it is not there!

Traditionally, the people of this town relied on agriculture for its economy. This worked well and would continue to do so. However, many new faces were showing up in town due to the center. This was the beginning of a problem.

Not being a very diversified economy, there were no jobs for these folks... and little housing. The new people were determined they were going to be a part of their new home, even if they had to continue living in campers and tents. They were not leaving.

The locals were pleased that the center was becoming so popular, and they welcomed the new people as much as they could. After Reverend Harry's talk, they now had an idea how they could integrate all these new people.

Wood made from combining organic waste material and recycled plastic became boards!

A solution that would eventually answer a large part of both problems. A site was selected, and the factory roared into life. Very soon, the boards were piling up in huge piles waiting for some construction to start.

The need for plastic became so great, they had to reach out to other nearby cities to keep the supply going.

---

Rose finally got to join in on new projects. Her job was to head up a committee to select the land for the new houses to be built upon. After all, when one works with Mother Nature, it is important to get input from her where she is willing to have her way disrupted.

Rose and her new committee gathered with their bicycles, ready to do a tour of the local area. To keep it fun, they planned a picnic on the site they would designate for the new homes. The other members, not being up on the ways of nature, wondered how they would know where this site would be. Rose just smiled as she rode off on her bike.

Everyone was having a wonderful time. It had been a long time since they had just wandered about their town aimlessly on bicycles. Some had even forgotten why they had gathered... until-

On the edge of town, an area of land that was mostly grass, with a light smattering of deciduous trees seemed to be dying. Normally, in mid-summer, the area was pristine with tall green wild oats and well-leafed trees, but today all the leaves drooped, brown, hanging lifeless from their limbs while the oats lay flat on the ground, also brown.

Teems of squirrels and mice scurried throughout the property, collecting the seeds from the oats. After all, nature abhors waste!

Rose looked at her committee members as they halted their bikes to look at the activity before them. "I presume this is the site that will be the home for the new houses. As we prepare all the materials, we can let the animals collect the grain and do whatever they wish for their part of the transition."

"I have an idea I would like to propose," stated one of the new folk, a woman of about forty who obviously was into nature and ecology. "I propose that instead of building several houses, we build a Co-housing complex much like a condo building. That way we can share resources better, use less space and live more communally. We should also look at incorporating Permaculture in the design of the total landscape. That way we can share better with Mother Nature."

Everyone agreed that Dawn's suggestions were exactly the way to go, so the wheels were now in motion.

"I happen to be an architect specializing in designing sites that accommodate the natural environment. I have some conceptual drawings of what I feel could happen in my motorhome."

Everyone was so excited by Dawn's offering that the picnic died on the spot. Getting back to the center became more like a race than a casual ride around town. Of course, Dawn arrived last because she had to swing by and get the papers.

# Chapter 26

With the approved plans in hand, construction could begin. Site preparation started once the animals had finished collecting their food. It was a little harder following the concept of permaculture, though, since all the plants had vacated the site. However, Dawn understood the lay of the land.

---

The construction crew was busy laying foundations one morning when a motorcade of cars showed up at the site.

"Who's in charge here?" yelled a big heavy-set man in an ill-fitting business suit, his fat belly hanging over his pants. "I am ordering this site to stop work. I am from the county engineering department. You cannot proceed without our blessings... and let me tell you, you do not have them."

Dawn walked up to the man and offered his hand, but the man just slapped the Stop Work order in his hand, then turned and walked away. Dawn tried to stop the man so they could talk, but all he saw was the motorcade vanish into the distance.

He turned to his crew. "You guys keep working. I am going back to the center to deal with this."

---

"It seems that we have ruffled some feathers with some folks at the capital because we have acted without recognizing their authority. They are planning to stall our project into non-existence, just to show us who is in charge.

We have methods for dealing with these situations though, so I suggest we have the workers spend their time doing parts of the project which will not aggravate the situation further and I will get things settled down with the capital people."

Rose then concluded the meeting by saying, "We have good methods for swaying minds."

---

Rose called in Goose and the other Wind Surfers. It was time for some special action!

They settled into meditation position, projecting their minds to the people who were causing the problem at the capital. As their minds entered the office, it felt like they were climbing into a sticky bag of guck. The energy was so congested and negative!

Not a concern to these folks, though. They focused their energies on washing the congested energy out of the area by visualizing a big white wave of water rushing into the building. Being that it was a psychic wave, no one got wet, but the intensity of it knocked a few of the bureaucrats right off their feet.

Sometimes people get comfortable in a situation that is not good for them, but they choose to stay there, anyway. They find themselves consoled by a limiting condition that serves no one at all. However, when these same folks encounter a huge white wave of Universal energy, it leaves them feeling naked and vulnerable.

Once the wave had washed away all the congested energy, Rose and her gang visualized a beautiful golden sun hovering over the people, letting its golden rays flow down, filling the void.

As the people absorbed the golden light, they relaxed. Some started crying, releasing old emotions, while some sat motionless. It felt like they had become paralyzed.

Soon, each one of them smiled. It looked almost like crocuses popping up from the ground in the spring. It was so wonderful to see. Rose and the gang grew huge smiles themselves as they felt the energy rise.

Soon, each member of the staff opened their eyes, got up, shook themselves off... and walked out the door (never to return).

Pulling their minds back to the center, Rose and the gang took the time to give thanks and to clean their own energy with the golden light. After all, one needs to have bright, shiny, and clean energy!

---

Returning to the worksite, Dawn was ready to dig in for real now. She did not know what had occurred at the Center, however, she felt very invigorated. She was not going to let some silly Stop Work Order impede progress on her new home.

It had been several days since the problem had manifested, but she felt everything was safe, so she gave orders to ramp up the construction. The footings were now in place for the residence, and the lumber from their factory was beginning to arrive.

As one truck was being unloaded, Dawn shook her head as she looked up the street. She groaned as she saw another cavalcade of cars approaching, but this time, she realized it was all motorhomes!

She scratched her head, wondering what was about to happen.

The motorcade screeched to a halt in front of the building site and the awful man who had served her notice stepped out of the first motorhome. Now Dawn was really scratching her head!

As the man walked up to her, he offered his hand. "I am sorry I was such a jerk last time. I felt I needed to be like that because I felt afraid that you would hurt me if I did not act tough.

Something happened when we got back to our office. We were all busy having coffee, avoiding our work, and gloating over how we had treated you, when all of a sudden, we felt something like a huge tide of water slam over us. It felt like all our fears were being washed away. Then we felt warm, like we had been sitting in the sun. It had been a long time since I had felt so good.

When we each opened our eyes, we realized we did not want to do this job anymore... so we quit.

We all met later and realized we needed to come to help you build your home and become a part of it... if you will let us."

Dawn beamed as he handed the man a shovel.

---

Construction moved along well. The weather had cooperated, so the build progressed on schedule, however, being a temperate rain forest climate, that second word had to happen at some point... and it did.

The rain started pouring down, making a swamp out of the construction site. It was pointless trying to work until the rain quit. That could be hours, days, or even months. Who knew?

Since the physical work could not continue, Dawn headed to the office at the Center. She whined a bit to Rose about the rain and how it was impeding the progress. Rose just smiled at her, and let her enjoy her whiney time.

When Dawn headed back outside and stopped dead in her tracks. It was not raining!

She headed back to the site. The puddles had drained, and the ground was dry. She shook her head as she called her fellow workers back.

They were as stunned as she was when they arrived at the construction site, because over at the campground, the rain was coming down in sheets!

Rose just laughed a little laugh as she looked out the window at the energetic dome she had created to keep the rain away. After all, the construction of the new buildings was a priority!

# Chapter 27

By the time they had completed the whole construction, there was not one co-housing building, but two. It was a good thing that the land of and around the site was owned by the city because by the time everything was complete; the plants had vacated 4 times as much land as the original site.

Dawn was beyond excited about this occurrence, even though she could not get her head around the how. This meant there was an opportunity to do organic permaculture gardening on the site. Her dreams were coming true, at last!

People were still showing up in town, wanting to be a part of whatever it was that was going on. Something was going to have to be done. There had been no intention of turning this little farming community into a city, but they just kept coming.

Rose called a meeting with Reverend Harry and all the Wind Surfers.

"We are so grateful that so many people are interested in our work, however, things are getting out of hand. This town will lose its character if it keeps growing at this pace. We need some suggestions to make a plan on how to put the cap on the bottle, so to speak. Anybody?"

Goose was quick to suggest that maybe they should do a survey of the people coming in. "We could find out where they are from, how many are in their group, and what was or was not going on at home that caused them to choose to vacate."

"That might be our only option," said Rose. "We cannot build a fence around the city to keep them out, and we do not want to send them away. So let's get pen and paper and go find out."

Smart alecks as ever, each of the Wind Surfers produced a smart tablet in their hands and set off to do the survey. Of course, the correct survey was already loaded, so all they had to do was punch yes or no with each person. Rose laughed and Reverend Harry shook his head... again.

---

It took several days to complete the survey. Every person asked was more than happy to take part, so sorting out this situation was easy.

The eventual outcome was very interesting. Every one of the newcomers suffered from the same situation... they were fed up with their lives. They just felt there was more than what their lives seemed to offer but did not know how to change it... until they learned about the center.

"So what can we do to help these people?" Reverend Harry asked as the meeting opened. "This is such a big problem. We need to help them, but they can't all live here. Besides, the people where they came from need help from them."

"I think another workshop is in order, to start with, but we may find that we need to set up a second center closer to their homes. It seems that an increasing desire for people to know themselves is causing this unrest. The old traditional life of growing up and working until you die isn't feeding the people anymore."

Workshops at the center are always open to everyone that wishes to participate; however, buildings have limitations. They are called walls. When the pending workshop was announced, so many people signed up they had to hold a lottery for seats, and offer several repeats.

Reverend Harry was now used to the large crowds of new people before him. He still preferred the old days of communing with his people in his church, but life had gotten much bigger, and Harry knew this was his place now.

Rather than standing at a podium lecturing, Harry placed a large comfy chair before the group on a raised platform. This was to be a guided discussion. Harry just hoped people would open up to him.

Before Harry could even open the discussion, a man was up on his feet. "We want to see changes in the way we live our lives. We feel the government is not listening to us. Things have become too expensive, so we have to work long hours just to feed our families. We don't know what else to do, so we have come here for help."

Harry smiled at the man, but before he could make a reply, a woman was on her feet. "This is the time for women to shine, but we are repressed by men. I want to have the freedom to do what I want; I don't want to be dictated to anymore."

The meeting was going sideways before it even had time to get started. As quickly as one person had their rant, another was on their feet. The meeting was into thirty minutes and Reverend Harry had not spoken a word. He was feeling flustered, but he sat and listened.

It was just never going to end. Did every one of the hundred or so people in attendance come here to complain? This was supposed to be an opportunity to enhance their lives.

He knew this meeting would never take place if he did not do something. Harry closed his eyes, took a deep breath, and began chanting. This was pretty weird because Harry had never chanted before. It did not faze Harry though, because he had gotten used to weird spontaneous things happening.

He continued to chant the Universal tone OM over and over. At first, the audience members continued to verbalize their complaints, ignoring the chanting. When they came to realize that no one was listening to them anymore, they became quiet. It was not long before some members of the audience began toning as well, then more... and more... and more until... everyone.

Harry continued the chant for several more minutes after the entire group had joined in. He could feel there was an energy level he needed to attain that would release the tension. Then the chanting stopped. All was quiet. One could feel the tension melting away as each person focused on their own breath.

Harry smiled, then after a few more minutes, he opened his eyes. Everyone remained quiet and in their seats, waiting for him to speak, but he did not.

Harry visualized a white cloud of energy filling the entire room. He continued visualizing it for several minutes while he took deep, positive breaths. At first, people were restless. They were not used to such quiet, but soon they started to enjoy what was happening. It felt like it had wrapped them in a warm, fuzzy blanket.

"How do you feel?" Harry began. No one spoke. They just smiled. Harry smiled as he realized he had connected with the crowd. He now understood the power of working as one with Cosmic energy.

"I hear the pain you felt earlier, but please realize and accept that it is all illusion. When you base your life on fear, you live in illusion.

When you learn to live in the joy of breathing in harmony with the Universe, the illusion melts away. As you let go, you will be able to not only see the truth, but you will know it, and live it.

Everyone, please take a deep breath, making sure you breathe from your belly. Hold it for a moment, then take your time, letting it out. Repeat this three times... Tell me how do you feel."

The woman who had earlier spoken of her issues about unfair treatment of women rose and spoke in a quiet tone. "I just cannot believe the difference in how I feel in just such a short time. I feel more solid, yet I can feel the energy around me like I am a balloon that is blown up to the max."

Everyone in the audience agreed, so Harry continued.

"We have been taught since before we were born to live in fear. It was not intentional; it was just a lack of understanding. Our parents just did not know. We now can understand this error... and we have, as you have shown today, the ability to do differently.

Once we begin to connect with Universal energy, the illusion weakens. We begin to see truth. Our minds open up to new information that supports our ability to make better decisions.

When we live our lives working long hours in jobs we may not enjoy, we are living in fear. We fear we can't live a lifestyle that our ego needs to sustain its perception of self-esteem. When we have to have the best home, the best car, a boat, and all the other trappings, we are avoiding our true selves because the ego is in control, so you think you need these things to feel happy.

I suggest to you it would be better if you were to become happy first, then decide what your life needs. I bet it will not be the same.

If you make the exercise we just did a regular part of your daily routine, you soon find that your life will change for the better. You will have better health, be more relaxed, happier. Teach everyone in your family to practice mindfulness and the tensions will melt away.

One woman raised her hand to speak, "Doesn't this philosophy you are espousing fly right against the teachings of our Church? I believe in the Christian God... and in Jesus."

Harry smiled for a long moment. "Jesus taught me this exercise." He paused for effect, to let what he had said sink in. The woman looked confused.

"The one thing I have learned in this transition is that we need to separate what is Church and what is God's teachings. What is the one thing God wants us to have... Love.

If your church, or any other organization, tries to teach you differently, they are teaching from the ego. The exercise we just completed brings you closer to a state of Agape love or Universal love. Love... and connection with everything and everyone."

A man this time, "What is the purpose of the ego, then? Is it all bad?"

"No, not at all. The ego has at least two important roles. The first is to ensure that you wake up as the same person each day. It might be a bit challenging if one day you know yourself as Suzy and the next you think you are George! The ego is your cyber wallet!

The second role is to protect you. When you are born, (with the exception of your personal karma), you have a clean slate; the exception being what you may have learned in vitro. The ego learns the rules to your life by observing as your life develops throughout your childhood. Once it learns the rules, it acts them out each time something happens that looks or feels similar to something that happened in your childhood... Good or bad. This will continue all your life... until something interrupts your programming that changes the rules... like what you experienced today.

Now you can start to recognize the false truths your ego runs on and change them. The first step is to connect with Spirit so you can attune to love. This gives you a base to work from.

By connecting with Source regularly, you will begin to notice, often by the feelings you get, when things are not right or not true for you. Once you recognize them as being false, you now have the opportunity to make changes.

This can be a tricky process because the ego does not like anyone messing with its power. It likes the way things are and may fight to keep things as they were. With patience, you will gain clarity allowing you to change the programming to something more suitable for you."

"But the Bible says we are sinners, and we just have to give our lives to Jesus to be saved," the same woman jumped up and threw at Harry.

Harry took a slow sip of water, then replied, "I realize some of the content of this conversation might feel threatening to some of you. Please let yourself feel the emotion, but try to stay open to what your mind tells you.

Men have translated the Bible through at least six languages since it was first put on paper. Men have rewritten many of the stories in the Bible to suit the concepts espoused by certain leaders. However, aside from this, the intent of the Bible still is valid. I invested over fifteen years as a minister here in this town. It was only when Jesus visited me in a dream that I came to realize that we are now in the timeframe that supports a new understanding of the Bible and other mystical treatises.

Our new teachings do not undermine the Bible, they expand on the concepts.

The most profound one for me, in fact, was the one that brought Jesus to me and, let me tell you, it threw my life into a tizzy, was John 1:16. Jesus said: I am The Way, The Light, and The Life.

In our previous incarnation, we interpreted this to mean that we just had to believe in Jesus and follow like mindless sheep, trusting our leaders to lead us to salvation. They led us to believe we were born bad, or sinners just for being human, and it was the duty of the clergy to help us be redeemed.

Our new understanding is that Jesus is our redeemer, but we are redeemed by becoming like Jesus. The new energy created by the Christ Consciousness leads us to do and be as He is. We are only sinners because we do not know. Like a brand new car, we need to be tuned up. The process of Redeeming is our tune-up.

When we recognize it is the lessons we assumed in our childhood that need to be changed, and we take action to change them, it enacts the process of Redemption.

By attuning through meditation, we are doing the Way to the Light, which brings us to the second phase, the Life. I, myself, all of a sudden, began doing healing work, just like Jesus. It was healing work beyond my greatest dreams. The question for each of you now is; what will your life look like when you let go of the ego control?

We each have a significant purpose in our lives. You have come to our fair town to learn life can be different from the ways of old. Take a moment to go inside and reflect on what inspires you."

Just like someone rang the dinner bell, several members of the audience stirred, like they needed to get somewhere. Then, the woman who had spoken before stood up. "I, for one, am going back home. I understand, at least somewhat, what you say. To embody this new perspective, I need to help my friends and family and grow from that.

And with that, the audience disappeared out the door. The road out of town was very busy!

Rose came in to see Harry still sitting in his chair. She smiled at him, looking around the empty room with a perplexed look on her face.

"Must have been something I said," laughed Harry.

# Chapter 28

"Have you ever heard of the Hundred Monkey syndrome, Goose?"

Reverend Harry and Goose were sitting in the kitchen of the Center having tea, relaxing after enjoying a wonderful yoga class. They were glowing in the light of the success of the Center. One could count on the fingers of one hand how many locals had not taken part in at least one program at the center. It was a different life for these folks, from those not so long ago days of fear and trauma.

"No, tell me about it, please."

The story goes that a monkey who lived with his tribe on an island off the coast of China decided one day that he should wash his fruit before eating it, so he picked the one he was going to eat then wandered down to a nearby stream and proceeded to wash it.

Other monkeys watched him, then saw how much more he enjoyed his meal, so they began washing their food as well. Soon, every monkey in the tribe washed their food each time before eating it. Upon the hundredth monkey choosing to wash his food, all the monkeys on nearby islands also began to wash their food. That is the hundred monkey syndrome."

"Cool," answered Goose, "I am going to tell the other guys"... and off he went before Reverend Harry could tell him why he wanted him to know about it.

A couple of days later, Reverend Harry was puttering around in the Center when Goose walked in.

"Why did you leave without letting me finish the other day? I wanted to discuss something with you."

"Oh." Goose stopped in his tracks. "I was so excited about seeing the monkeys that I got the other Wind Surfers together and we went to see them."

"You went to see the monkeys? They live on remote islands off the coast of China. How did you do that? Is this something else I don't need to know, Goose?"

Goose just laughed. "What did you want to discuss with me, Reverend Harry?"

"The Hundred Monkey syndrome is a concept that people in the human training industry aim for. They want enough people to accept and practice their teachings that the concepts become a natural part of their lives.

Driving cars would be an example of social manipulation that has become a social norm. It has become embedded in the social consciousness, so it is now a natural part of life. If you go back to the early 20th Century, people did not know how to drive cars. They would have to think step by step about how to incorporate the strategies and rules required to operate a motor vehicle.

Fifty years later, small children can operate ride-em cars by the time they are three.

What I am pointing to here is that we need to aim for our concepts to become accepted and practiced by enough people that the hundred monkey syndrome kicks in. Then the evolution of humanity will explode!"

"I think we are well on our way, Reverend Harry. Now that you presented your workshop to those folks here at the Center, we are hearing a lot of feedback that they have changed their lives. Folks around here are sure happier and more fulfilled too!

What are you thinking we might do to move things along a little quicker? I know you well enough to know this is not a casual conversation," Goose laughed.

"I am thinking it is time for the Wind Surfers to do a road trip. Music, especially your music, is a great way to engage people to embrace change. What do you think?"

Before Goose could even answer, seven more people were sitting in on the discussion.

Condor laughed, "I guess we have our own kind of hundred monkeys. They were pretty cool, by the way. Would you like to see them, Reverend Harry?"

Harry just laughed his nervous laugh. Although each day brought something new to stretch his limitations, he was not ready to go see the monkeys... yet.

So they created plans for the road trip. The first concert, of course, was to be right here in the park where it all began. When word got out about the concert, the people in the town went into a real tizzy. Everyone was so excited. Knowing what happened in the past, the town was silent for several days before the concert date... everyone was sleeping! They knew there would be no time for such trivial things once the music started.

---

By the time the concert was ready to start, the park was past standing room only, so people parked their vehicles, blocking all the nearby roads. More room for dancing!

The entire town, including the newbies, stood anticipating the first song... and they were off. For three solid days, the music played on. The Wind Surfers played and played, never repeating one song. They just played what inspired them.

They created every song to inspire heartfelt love and happiness... and most important... connection with Source. By the end of the concert, everyone was floating... literally!

Now that the easy concert was history, the Wind Surfers were off to their first untested location. Lucky for them, it was the city where many of their recent visitors were from. Since the members of the group had never experienced rejection, they had no reservations about playing there. They just knew people would love them and their music.

They arrived at the designated park the day before the concert was to begin. No one had done anything to organize or promote the event. People were just milling around the park, like any other day.

"I guess we have to turn the power on ourselves," laughed Condor.

"Let's do a visualization here to set the energy of manifestation. We know we are going to have a great time here tomorrow with the park filled to the brim with the right people."

---

They arrived at the park the next morning. It was Saturday, so the music would start in the early afternoon. The park still showed no signs of organization. Mentally noted, but knowing how to not get hung up about such a minor issue, the Wind Surfers began preparing for the concert on their own.

Manifesting a stage was no big deal, and since none of their instruments (including their electric guitars) required electricity, there was nothing else to set up. Well, except for the food trucks, of course.

The time for the concert came, and nobody showed up.

Oh well, they were here to play a concert and they will play.

1,2,3,4 and the music began. They were hot today, the music just rolled out into the ethers. The patrons in the park just continued with their walks and picnics without notice of the music.

Papi decided enough was enough! She would get their attention.

Becoming her Golden Butterfly, she flew over the people. As she moved to the music, she hovered over some small children nearby and even landed one little girl's nose.

The little girl's laughter was the button that turned the people on. When her mother saw the butterfly land on her daughter's nose, she laughed so hard, she dropped her cell phone (OMG). Reaching for it, her ears opened up. She realized there was music playing.

Grabbing her daughter, she ran over to the music and began clapping and dancing like a crazy person. Now there was hope!

Papi continued cajoling the people in the park until she had amassed a sizable crowd. Thinking to herself, "We need a hundred people, we need a hundred people." She kept flying back and forth, counting the attendees... and miraculously, when the hundredth person showed up, the park exploded. The party was on... and the food trucks, almost like a miracle, arrived with yummy treats for everyone. Goose smiled.

As the music played, each musician scanned the audience, looking for the people who had visited their town in the recent past. They could see no one.

The people at the concert became mesmerized by the music. They heard the messages inside each song. Their energy changed as the concert played on, relaxing, expanding, strengthening. But where were the people they had expected?

After they had played for several hours, they noticed a large crowd entering the park with a lady leading them. As the crowd approached the musicians, they realized it was the woman from the workshop who had been complaining about women being treated as lesser humans.

She walked straight up onto the stage with her followers, who formed a line across the front with their backs to the audience and just glared. She seemed to have concerns!

People on the ground never noticed them. They were too busy dancing. The musicians just smiled and carried on playing. The intruders stood their ground until, at last, the music got to them. At first, it was just a little wiggle and a sidestep, then they forgot why they had intruded to start with. Without leaving the stage, they lost themselves in the songs. Papi was having a ball, dancing, or more correctly flitting and twirling, hypnotized like a whirling dervish overhead!

These people had not heard about the three-day concerts, so once evening approached they began to fade away until all that remained were the folks on the stage, but even they stopped dancing. Soon, the concert was done.

The woman smiled at the Wind Surfers, then said, "We can see right through you people, this cult you are trying to drag people into. I spoke with our pastor about you guys. He told us to stay clear because you people just say pretty words that hold no real truth. He told me they excommunicated Reverend Harry from his church when he joined your cult."

Before anyone could say anything else, the woman and her followers marched right off the stage.

---

That night, as the woman tossed and turned in her bed. She had a dream. A beautiful Angel hovered over her and said: "*I am Rachel. I serve the Universal God that created this earth and all that exists. I invite you to join me in this moment of knowing yourself through the eyes of God.*"

Even though the woman slept, she looked Rachel right in the eyes, then wept.

The next night, Rachel returned. The woman wept again. For five nights, Rachel reached out to the woman. but each time she resisted listening to her. On the fifth night, Rachel reached down and stroked the woman's hair, trying to calm her down.

At last, the woman opened up while still sobbing, "I know who you are, and I know what you are going to say, but I am so afraid to turn against my religion. You must go!"

Rachel then reached out to the leader of the woman's church. She said: "*I am Rachel. I serve the Universal God that created this earth and all that exists. I invite you to join me in this moment of knowing yourself through the eyes of God.*"

The minister looked at her and laughed. "You do not exist in the eyes of my ministry; therefore, you must return to where you came. You will not drag me into your phony game."

Again, Rachel turned away.

The minister returned to his sleep. He began dreaming about a snake. It was a huge viper that was so big that its giant head peered down on him as it lay coiled nearby. The viper told him he must go to the Center and talk with Rose.

The dream occurred again and again until at last; he sought Rose.

Rose had prepared herself to meet him when he arrived. He felt furious, mostly because of lack of sleep, but he felt so angry, almost irrational. First, an angel tried to talk to him in his sleep, then a gigantic snake threatened him if he did not speak to this Tarot Card reader.

Rose pleasantly smiled at him as he made himself comfortable. He tried to act like he was only seeing her to make the dream go away, but deep down inside, it intrigued him. Rose offered him a lovely cup of hot tea, then she sat and waited for him.

It did not take long for the Destiny Tea to do its job. The man was soon staring at his future self. This time, as he turned to look back, he saw two paths. The first one was his current path. It was filled with emptiness and despair. On the other path, he saw a man like himself that emanated an energy so brilliant he could not look at him. He turned back to look at his future self and all he heard was the word- Choose.

He sat there for a long while, knowing which he must choose, but his ego was determined to make its own choice. He cracked as he began to cry. The tears were just a trickle at first, but then he broke down and sobbed. Rose sat across from him and waited.

Not being able to make a clear decision, he made none. He opened his downcast eyes, unable to look at Rose. He remained this way for several minutes. Rose sat without expression, watching him.

Rachel appeared in the room, floating behind Rose. She smiled at the man. When he saw her, he sat straight up and gasped.

"You are the Angel from my dream. Why do you haunt me?"

"*I am Rachel. I serve the Universal God that created this earth and all that exists. I invite you to join me in this moment of knowing yourself through the eyes of God.*

*You have been given the opportunity to know yourself and to become all that you can be. Yet, you make no choice. I ask you now, do you choose to know yourself in truth through the eyes of God, or do you choose to continue to live controlled by your ego?*

*How can you serve your people if you cannot make this decision?*"

"I serve my people in the best way I know how, according to my understanding of our Bible. My people need me to guide them, to keep them from making errors, such as praying to the wrong God. The God I know tells me how to lead them, and this mockery is not his doing. I choose the first path."

With that, the man rose and stormed out of the office. When he arrived back at his church, several officious-looking people greeted the man.

"Are you the minister of this church?" one visitor asked him.

Upon indicating yes, they told him he was under arrest for embezzlement. They had seized the church's records that were now to be audited. With that, the arresting officer placed a padlock on the door of the church, leaving the little church abandoned.

Upon hearing of the minister's arrest, the woman got on her knees and prayed. She no longer knew what to believe.

Rachel appeared before her, smiling, but saying nothing. She opened her arms to invite her in. Her heart shone bright like the sun, filling the woman's heart with loving energy as she remained in supplication.

Then the woman looked up at Rachel with tearful eyes. Remaining quiet, she just stared at the glowing angel before her.

*"Let your heart guide you, my dear Asha. As your name implies, it is time for you to shine. Take the time to shake off that which no longer belongs and breathe in the very life you were born to express."*

# Chapter 29

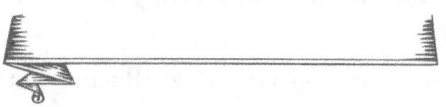

The gang felt a little shaken by the outcome of their first concert on new ground. It was a new lesson for them. In all their lives, they had felt nothing but absolute love and acceptance.

Returning to the Matrix, they found solace inside their cedar trees. As they dreamed, they each asked the same question:

"Why would people choose to live their lives away from God?"

As they dreamed, they saw a man standing before an enormous pile of bananas. He took each banana and attempted to open it. If the banana opened with ease, it released a little angel who flew off into the light.

When a banana resisted being opened, he placed it on a table next to him where it was bathed in warm sunlight. Later, he would try to open the banana once more. If it opened up, a little angel would fly off.

The man soon found he had an enormous pile of unopened bananas. He smiled and waited as the sunlight shone on them. After a long time, some of the bananas did indeed ripen enough for an angel to appear and take flight. Many did not ever open.

---

The Wind Surfers settled into their virtual room the next morning.

"What do you think the dream was about?" asked Raven.

"Free choice," answered Papi.

"Reincarnation, or more accurately Rebirth," said Phoenix.

As the discussion continued, Oona appeared. At first, no one noticed her as she sat and listened, and then, like a magnet thrown into a pile of iron filings, she found herself covered with eight bodies. They hugged her like she had never been hugged before.

Settling down, with faces smiling like the sun, they almost broke into tears. Oona attempted to speak to them as she cried in joy.

"My beloved friends, it is with the greatest joy that I see you again. You are in my heart and mind always.

Please accept the lesson from this situation as a vision of the work we are still to do. Humans are born with Spirit inside them. It may take many lifetimes for them to realize and accept that the outer banana is not reality, but an illusion. Throughout their existence, there are opportunities to release themselves from the illusion. They can then become one with the Light of God, but if the banana has not evolved enough, it cannot hear the calling of its soul."

"What happens to the bananas that do not open up?" asked Papi.

"I have heard people talk about some place called hell. Do they go there?" asked Condor.

"Part of the illusion is this place called hell. It is, in fact, not a place, but a being. The soul itself knows its purpose is to grow and release itself from burdens it has outgrown. This may take many, many lifetimes. Hell is when the soul knows it needs to grow to release itself, but either can't or won't, so it suffers from the disconnection this resistance causes.

Humans have even created a character who is claimed to be powerful like their God, who can prevent them from entering heaven if they make a mistake. Strange enough, they have created their picture of this character from the mythical god, Pan, the keeper of nature.

They are taught they need to live in guilt. They need to pay penance for not being perfect in each learning opportunity provided, and that they need to give up their power to evolve and make new choices. This is hell! One does not have to die to go to hell, one just has to choose to refuse to open one's eyes to the light!

As long as a banana refuses to ripen, it will just sit there asleep waiting for the light to be absorbed so it can ripen. Some take a very long time!

The most important aspect of this lesson for us is to realize that we have done our best to provide an opportunity for people to grow. It is their free choice to join in or not. We need to just keep playing the music!"

---

The next concert was ready to go. It was going to be in the town where they had quelled the riots so many years ago. This will be interesting!

When they arrived at the site, they realized they were going to be playing in the same park as before. The food trucks were even there already!

Goose was in his zone on this job! He loved to eat. It made his day just knowing the food trucks were here already. "I might have to write a song about my love for food trucks!" he laughed to himself.

Since everything was ready to go, they walked up onto the stage to prepare, only to turn around to face an audience of over one thousand excited fans. Now, this was going to be fun. It was party time!

The party became too large for the park, so people began spilling into the street. Since it was surrounded by busy streets, they could not block them off, so Papi, dawning her wings, flew off to find a nearby park.

Recognizing the beach where they had camped and partied at an earlier time, she flew back. As fast as a thought, she relayed the information to everyone. That fast, the Wind Surfers were playing up a storm to several thousand people who did not notice the gang was playing in two separate venues... at the same time!

No one seemed concerned at all, as long as the music continued.

For three wonderful days, they shut the city down as all the people partied and partied. All was well, until a few days after life returned to normal when the local newspaper contained pictures of both parties, with guess who right in the middle?

The local populace did not seem to care. They had had a fine time and were feeling strangely better about their lives. However, several of the local clergies were a little disconcerted, to say the least.

"What kind of trickery is this? How can the band be in two places at once? Humans can't do that. They must have a cover band that looks similar to them," a very narrow-minded minister muttered to himself. "I had better look into this. I heard those songs they were singing. We cannot condone songs that undermine what our churches stand for."

---

The newspaper was sitting on a table in the kitchen when Condor wandered in looking for some breakfast. He glanced at it as he walked by, stopping in his tracks.

When Goose came in a few minutes later, Condor laughed and told him to look at the front page of the paper.

"Pretty cool eh, got us in two places. That should help the monkeys!" he said.

"I hope they think that is our cover band, Condor. There may be people who might become scared if they think we can be in two places at once. We need to cover this up in a hurry!"

By the time they were finished looking at the newspaper, all the Wind Surfers were in the room. Goose stressed to them the seriousness of this situation. They had to come up with a viable solution.

Raven suggested, "Maybe there are people in the third group that look similar enough to us that we can dress up to make a cover story for us. But how are we going to cover Papi?"

Raven looked again at the picture. One had to look really close to even see Papi. He then focused on the second picture, visualizing only seven band members. It took a little time, but then he smiled in relief.

"Look at the pictures again. They are not the same anymore."

The others looked and agreed. No Papi in the second photo. They searched around to see if there was a second copy of the paper lying anywhere. None to be found, so Raven popped over to a newsstand nearby and grabbed one. No, Papi in the second picture. His projection had worked.

"Let's get back to planning our next gig, people. We had better lie low for a while until the wind settles. This next session will be in a town where we have no history, so let's hope none follows us there."

---

The next concert was in place for the coming weekend. This gave them all a chance to lie low and recharge their batteries. Lots of cedar tree time!

Saturday morning, they arrived at the designated site. Their history was indeed already following them. There were thousands of anxious fans milling about the park. When the people saw them, they rushed at them like love-crazed teenagers.

The gang put up a calming energy field around themselves so that by the time the crowd reached them, they had become manageable. They smiled at each other as they walked up onto the stage.

Before they could start playing, a newspaper writer, who had pushed his way up to the front, yelled at them, "Hey, were you guys really in two places at once?"

Goose smiled at him and cautiously replied, "If you look, the pictures are different. There are only seven people in the second. Would you like to meet our cover band?"

And with the snap of a finger, seven identical figures walked up onto the stage, waving and smiling at the crowd.

The newspaper writer stepped back, caught off guard. As he moved away, he realized there had been no one at the foot of the stairs previous to their introduction. He kept walking away, but now he was determined to get to the bottom of this mystery.

# Chapter 30

**"I** can't believe how much power I had given away to that man, and I cannot believe how wonderful I feel now, so liberated. Thank you, Reverend Harry," Asha said as they shared tea.

Asha had become a regular participant at the Center since her life after the minister's arrest had been turned upside down.

"We are glad to have you with us. You seem to be much more comfortable with yourself, Asha. That is always good.

I have something I would like to discuss with you since we have the time today, my friend. I hope you feel comfortable enough with me to discuss it. Are you familiar with a concept called addictive personalities?"

Asha nodded, but looked down at her lap, feeling very uncomfortable.

"All people have unconscious beliefs they developed in their childhood that inhibit their ability to function in their best possible way as adults, at least until they are recognized and reframed.

The purpose of these core beliefs is to protect the person as they move through their lives. Some people need to dominate, while others retreat at the slightest hint of threat. Some people feel afraid to be alone, so they need to belong to something, so they feel they have an identity. Do you know anyone like that?"

Asha sat staring at Reverend Harry. She knew what he was saying. "It is true. I have always felt the need to be a part of something. I feel empty when I am not part of a group. Is that wrong?"

"No, the belonging is a part of being human. We all have a natural tendency to commune. However, when the need to be a part overrides the ability to think and discern for one's self, or one's own needs, it becomes a protective device. Coping methods such as this stem from one's feeling of abandonment as a child.

The reason I bring this up today is my desire for you to truly know and be your powerful self. We love and welcome you as a part of the force that is developing from the Center. However, if you are only here because you need somewhere to belong, you will never reach your full potential. Can you accept this, Asha?"

Asha gulped, searching for a lifeboat. She knew this was a life-changing moment. Her shoulders dropped as her feelings of abandonment rushed out of her mind.

Reverend Harry reached over and took her hand. "It is okay to feel the way you do right now. Just remember, you are not your memories or the attached feelings. If you are ready to let go of this feeling, let's do a visualization.

Asha took a deep breath, then sat up straight, closing her eyes.

"Visualize yourself sitting on a chair in the back of your mind, Asha. In front of you, at the front of your mind, is what we call the Screen of Your Mind.

Let yourself relax and continue taking deep, positive breaths. Allow your memories of abandonment to show on the screen. Let yourself feel how what it is like to be abandoned.

Now, see above your head a beautiful yellow sun shining down, pouring warm rays of sunlight into the image on your screen. Let the sun's rays wash away the feelings of abandonment until all you are looking at is a picture, just a picture.

Now, let the sunlight fill the picture on your screen with warmth and love. Keep doing positive breathing to fuel the sunlight.

Enjoy the feelings that are now developing in the scene. Hold them for a moment, then let them go, letting your screen go blank.

Sit in silence for a few moments. Then take one more deep breath and come back to the room."

"I had a twin sister when I was born. She only lived for a few days. I have missed her all my life. My parents thought I was being ridiculous since she died before I was old enough to even know her. But I did know her, and she is still with me today. This is the first time I have sensed happiness in my life."

Harry took her hand again, smiling, and said, "Let's do one more visualization then."

Asha got herself ready and off they went again.

"On the screen of your mind, invite your sister to join you. Let her express herself as she wants you to see her. Just relax and let it happen.

When she is there, reach out to her and see what happens."

Asha screamed in delight. She got to hug her sister. A lifelong desire was now satisfied.

"Ask your sister why she left so soon after being born, Asha."

Asha replied, "She was only meant to live for this short time. It was part of my life purpose to work through abandonment, so I could attain my best personal power. It saddened her as well to leave, but it was the way it needed to be. Now that we are back together, we can embrace each other in full. I will never be alone again."

Asha took a deep breath and opened her eyes. She jumped up and shocked Reverend Harry by giving him a big hug.

"I now understand what you want me to realize. I can be powerful on my own. Being a part of this work makes me happy. This process has helped me live a more fulfilled life. A lifetime of sadness, gone in a flash. Thank you, Reverend Harry."

"Thank the Universe. I am only the channel, my dear. Now, there is one more visualization if you are up to it."

Once again, Asha sat and closed her eyes, ready to take on the world.

"Watch the screen of your mind once again, Asha. This time, let a picture of your life purpose show on the screen."

"I am going to open a second training Center in the building that used to be our church. It is time to go home." With that, Asha gave Reverend Harry one more hug, and she bolted for the door.

---

Guardian Angel Rachel smiled from above as Asha sat in her car in front of what used to be her church. Asha stared at the already converted building, ready for the next part of her journey.

# Chapter 31

The Hundred Monkey syndrome had indeed come to be. They filled every concert to the max... mostly with the same people.

The gang sat in the yoga room at the Matrix, relaxing after another successful three-day concert. One would think it would elate them that the concerts were going off so well, but they were not. In fact, they were feeling a little frustrated.

"I thought the concerts were meant to elevate people's consciousness so they would become more connected with Source. It seems they are only more connected with us," Raven said to start the session.

"Yes, it seems that they, in particular, our groupies, are not getting the message, although they do look shinier."

"What do we need to do differently, then? It must be how we are setting the stage, so to speak. Let's have a quiet time so we can all focus on the situation and see what pops up," suggested Condor.

It only took a few minutes of pondering to come up with the answer.

In unison, they all said, "We need to change the intention."

"We have lost our focus; we have just been having fun. The great thing is that we have got a lot of monkeys washing their food now, which was our intention. Now we need to focus on getting them to understand our raison d'être... our reason for being!

"And that is an easy fix, guys," laughed Goose.

Before the next weekend's concert began, they agreed they needed to do a visualization to set the stage for them. This concert was going to shift a lot of minds and lives.

This was going to be exciting!

And sure enough, the change in focus worked. Their groupies realized the shift, at least from an unconscious level. It was easy to see the shift in their energies all the way from the stage. They glowed.

And... they kept dancing too, but now they spread themselves out so they could connect with other new people dancing. As they twisted and shouted, they encouraged their new dance partners to open up and hear what the music was telling them.

They were well into the evening when a man, a man with an obvious agenda, walked right up on the stage. He did not even wait for their song to finish. He just took the microphone and began talking.

"I am from the city licensing office. I hereby terminate this concert. Please leave the area."

The music ground to a halt, the people stopped dancing. The one thing the man did not count on came next. As he stepped off the stage, a crowd surrounded him.

They were not angry, and they did not touch him. However, they were not going to let him stop the party and just leave. They just blocked his path and focused on him, breathing positive breaths and sending him loving thoughts.

Then, he turned and walked back up on the stage, took the mike, and said, "What the heck, let's party!"

And with that, he ripped off his coat and tie and threw himself out into the audience in a belly flop. Lucky for him, many people knew what he was doing, so they banded together to catch him. He landed on the ground, already dancing! (He quit his job the next work day!)

# Chapter 32

The change in intention was exactly what had been needed. In the following months, Asha had a lot of new company. New centers were springing up all over the place.

Rachel beamed as she helped transform redundant buildings into shiny new training facilities from her nest in the sky. Only by Cosmic will did the right group of people appear to create each new center. They came together with only the desire to help others move forward.

The Hundred Monkeys were now in the thousands. People were flocking to the centers, having heard the messages inside the songs of the Wind Surfers that had inspired them. People kept telling the folks running the Centers they wanted genuine change. Their lives had begun to show the happiness they felt as they began shedding the lies they had lived with for so long.

The Wind Surfers kept playing week after week to keep up the momentum. It was a good thing they were always in a state of rejuvenation. It was like they were in an energetic bath that washed over and into them all the time. These non-stop concerts would have worn out anybody else after the first concert, which was now so long ago. These amazing guys just took it in stride and kept the music flowing... and the band played on.

Every concert provided new and inspiring music for the ever-swelling crowds. The Wind Surfers were so used to just popping in and playing each gig; they stopped looking into the crowds to see who they were attracting.

The newspaper reporter hid under a distant tree. He had gone unnoticed for quite some time as he continued his regimen of taking pictures and making notes. It wasn't until Papi went for a little fly-by over the crowd they became aware of him carrying out his covert activities.

It was not the most fortunate timing, (maybe), that the reporter had been watching the activities on the stage when Papi transitioned. He just about bit through his pen when she popped into her Golden Butterfly. Now, his determination to get to the bottom of all this was lit into a bonfire.

He made sure he was hanging around when the event was over. Once again, the Wind Surfers had pulled off a raucous three-day event without taking a break for anything. He, himself, had gone home twice to sleep and still felt exhausted at the end.

When the concert was over, they did not let the reporter sneak off. As the music wrapped up, Condor sent a message out into the minds of the partiers that they wanted the reporter invited up to the stage.

At first, he tried to get away, but who can say no to five hundred people surrounding you? They all locked their arms tight, interlocking with each other in rows and rows around the man, smiling like friends as they stared at him.

The crowd then transitioned their posturing into a long double line and invited him to walk up to the stage. Goose was there to invite him up. Before he hit the top step, he was already a changed man. Being saturated with all that positive, loving energy from the crowd, he found peace in himself.

Once the crowd had disbursed, Goose invited him to sit with him. Legs hanging over the edge of the stage, Goose asked him what he would like to know.

Shaking like he had Parkinson's Disease, he pointed at Papi, asking "How did she do that?" Then he looked at Goose, "How do you play for three days solid without even taking a bathroom break? Who are you people?"

Goose smiled at him, saying nothing for a moment.

"Would you like to visit our Center? You can drive there in only a few hours. You can even stay for a few days if you have time. We need to get packed up for now, so if you would like to head off, we will meet you there."

---

As he pulled up to the curb in front of the Matrix, Goose walked out to greet him. "How the....? was all he could mumble. When Goose reached out to shake his hand, he almost fainted.

Sheila and Beth were busy in their office when Goose and the man came in. Sitting down like a man floundering in a dream state, he was nearing a nervous breakdown, waiting for the next unexplainable thing to happen.

Beth smiled at him, offering him a nice cup of hot tea. It was not long before the answers flowed, as his destiny was offered to him.

Finally, (not like there is ever an end to this!) Rachel appeared above him saying,

"*I am Rachel. I serve the Universal God that created this earth and all that exists. I invite you to join me in this moment of knowing yourself through the eyes of God.*

*As you have seen in recent days, life is not always what you see believe. If you choose to accept your destiny, you will be of great service to the Universal God and to your unlimited self. It is time that the mysteries you have seen before you will be presented to all. After all, there really are no mysteries, only truths unknown.*"

When he opened his eyes, he remained quiet for quite some time. Gone was the angry, determined reporter. In his place was a quiet man, pondering.

"Managing your public image is a monumental task for the long term," Frank told the meeting. "Attempting to manage growth like you have seen already without a plan in place is a road to certain disaster."

Frank not only had a full tour of the Matrix, but he also found his own bed there. He was like a man who had been rescued from a sinking ship. He knew himself well enough and thought he was on track, but deep down inside, he knew there was more, much more.

The Wind Surfers kept their concert dates up, the crowds kept swelling, the centers kept sprouting up. They were being noticed, to say the least.

One of the great attractions to the concerts was that no one knew anything about this band. They just appeared, played, and disappeared.

They had already had three occasions where people had interfered in their fun... there was a good possibility there would be more! So far, these intrusions had found happy endings. Frank found his place in ensuring they stayed that way.

They decided that Reverend Harry's Center would become headquarters for their work. Now they just needed to build the staff.

"Is this the HQ for the Wind Surfers Band?" the man asked as he interrupted the meeting. "I heard there might be an opportunity for me to join in."

The gang recognized him as the man who had tried to shut down their concert a few weeks ago. It seems that bellyflopping off the stage had been a good action for him!

"How did you know to come here?" asked a surprised Frank. "We are just talking about increasing our management staff this very moment."

"A voice in my head told me to come here this morning. I did not even know where here is. I just got in my car, and it pretty well drove itself here. So, here I am. I want to be a part of this. My name is Mel."

Rose smiled at Mel, offering him a lovely cup of sweet tea.

---

The concert crowds kept becoming bigger and bigger. The gang traveled further and further from their home. Much of the crowd followed them from week to week. They were getting noticed.

---

"What if we were to make a cartoon movie about the antics of the Wind Surfers?" Frank suggested during a morning coffee meeting one day. "That would up the ante with getting the word out. I have some contacts in the industry that could make this happen."

"If they can write it in such a way that the message got out there in the tone we are offering it, it might be a good way to go. That way, people overseas can get in on it too," agreed Raven.

"My concern is that the concerts are becoming so popular that someone who does not like our message might try to interfere. At least if they make it into a movie, there would be little they could do. After all, the concerts, albeit fun, are not essential to getting the message out. Correct?" offered Mel.

---

It took a lot of digging around, but they found success, so the cartoon movie came to be. Their biggest challenge in creating it was not finding people to produce it, but forcing them to include the messages. The dark side of the movie industry had a hidden agenda, so they wanted to make the movie a spoof, interested only in making money. Persistence paid off.

The movie was a hit as soon as they released it. All over the world, people were rushing to theaters, sometimes having to be forced out after enjoying it back to back several times.

People worldwide were hungry for spiritual knowledge. They wanted the truth, the actual truth, the kind that can only come through a quiet mind and an open heart. "The Ascenders" movie was doing its job.

The concerts continued. People still wanted to dance and enjoy the essence of the music. It was becoming apparent, though, that it was time to focus on a new project. So soon, the concerts stopped.

At first, the regulars were unhappy that they ended the parties in the park. They vented in newspapers. Radio announcers pondered who these people were and how come they had never been on their radar. However, at the end of the day, the parties were gone.

It worked to their benefit that no one seemed to see the relationship between the band and the spread of all the new spiritual centers. No one noticed that the centers, now operating to full capacity all over the country, had sprung into existence in each town right after the Wind Surfers held their concerts.

The members of the band were very careful to only project an introduction of the centers into the minds of the dancers, mentioning nothing about themselves.

# Chapter 33

"I need to get to the bottom of this! Attendance in my churches has dropped to record lows and my ministers are being questioned like never before," muttered the minister. He had built a sizable fortune in providing Christianity to his flock. More than a dozen churches, all in the cities where the Wind Surfers had played.

He called a meeting of his council. This was likely to become a war council. He was not a happy camper!

"Weren't these the same people that quieted the city down that was rioting a couple of years ago? If they are, they sure have a good technique. Even the police and members of the city council joined in. They must have some information about who these people are," suggested one committee member.

Before long, they pulled a plan together. Each person was going to investigate a related event to see if they could get any information at all.

When they reconvened a week later, there were several very perplexed-looking faces at the table. Not one clue had become evident.

One member stated, "I even talked to the food truck people at the event. They told me no one invited them. They just got an urge to drive over near the park and soon found themselves the busiest they have ever been."

"Well, I spoke to the members of that city council and got the same response. They were so happy to see the riots melt away that it never occurred to them to ask who these people were," offered another.

"I went to some of these new centers this week," stated the head minister. "I expected to be turned away, but instead, they were very kind to me and offered me some free courses. They told me that Jesus had spoken to them and gave them specific instructions about creating the centers!

Really! He has never told me anything, for as long as I have been a minister. You would think being a minister of my high standing that Jesus would be talking to me, not some lay people off the street!"

So, by the end of the meeting, they had concluded nothing, but the head minister was not one to quit. These people were interfering in his parish, and his income flow.

---

Mel hurried to the Matrix, looking for Frank and anyone else he could find. He had some news that needed to be passed on, and quick. Entering the building, he found Beth busy working away at her desk. Upon listening to his news, she closed her eyes for a moment, took a deep breath, and about a minute later, all the Wind Surfers with Frank were sitting at the council table. Mel shook his head, then joined them.

"One of my city council friends over in that city where the riots were called me yesterday to tell me that a minister who is head of many local churches was in this week asking questions about the band who ended the riots. He was determined to get some answers. He got none and left quite perturbed.

This was part of my concern that caused me to join you. There is going to be a backlash from the church movements. They do not like having their flocks fed information from unapproved sources."

---

"You want me to what?" blurted out the regional police chief. "You want me to raid all of these new spiritual centers? And what do you want me to look for? I heard they like doing yoga. Do you want me to confiscate their yoga mats?"

The minister was not used to being spoken to in such a way, so he became very defensive, but he needed these centers closed. He must have something he can get on these people.

"We need some legislation to prohibit these kinds of centers. They are teaching blasphemy. They even told me Jesus told them how to construct these places. Maybe there is an old law still in force that has not been used for a long time that will help us."

The police chief told him he wanted no part of this business unless the minister could come up with a law that would give his officers reason to bother these people. As they ended their conversation, the police chief recalled Mike visiting him just before the riots ended. The chief shook his head and returned to the papers on his desk.

---

"Here is our route to terminating these centers for good," the minister told his council members.

"I had a lawyer friend look into archaic laws that can still be enforced today. He found us one that we are working on reviving. We are having Cease and Desist Orders placed on all these centers. Goodbye yoga!

He showed me the law. The government of the day created it well over a hundred years ago. It states that the church has the right to determine if an outside business or educational institute is undermining the teachings of the churches. We have already seen that this is true!

It also states that the perpetrators can be burned at the stake as heretics, but I am hoping they will be reasonable and just close their doors. If we have to get our matches out, though, we will!"

Soon after, on behalf of the minister, the lawyer made an application to court to have the law applied to the spiritual centers.

The judge, as it turned out, was also a friend of the minister's. He issued Cease and Desist Orders for all the centers without a further thought.

In the next week, a police officer visited every center with the paperwork to shut them down... however...

---

Ever-confident, Rachel watched the whole scenario unfold. She had no plans to interfere. She knew her people could work this little situation through to a successful conclusion.

Once the grapevine had enlightened them again, everyone involved met at Harry's Center. Frank and Mel were shining examples of trepidation, to say the least. As they sat bobbing around like spinning tops, the rest of the team just sat in their own calmness, smiling at them.

"I know you guys have a lot of tricks up your sleeve, but what are you going to do once this minister has all the Centers shut down? This kind of undermines all the great work that has been done."

When Mel was able to settle down, he drank his sweet tea, then found himself perplexed as he stared at a man who looked just like him. Mel looked back to where he pointed and saw his purpose. He also saw a beautiful Angel who smiled at him, as his fears melted from the scent of lavender.

*"I am Rachel. I serve the Universal God that created this earth and all that exists. I invite you to join me in this moment of knowing yourself through the eyes of God.*

*For us to complete our mission, I invite you to accept the challenge of allowing the Universe to guide you as we assist our friends in moving to the next level of their enlightenment."*

Mel smiled and opened his eyes.

"You people sure have some interesting helpers, and you sure have some different ways of fixing problems. I do not know what I can do to help, but I feel confident that this is where I need to be. What can I do to help?"

Due to the nature of this interaction, they decided that a ground-level recourse had to be applied. Mel visited the Bar Association the next day to get information on the lawyer and judge.

Through the Freedom of Information process, he discovered these two had acted together on several controversial situations, but they had never been brought before the board because they were skilled at maintaining discretion.

Once Mel requested an inquiry, the silence was ended.

Both the lawyer and the judge tried to have the inquiry quashed, however, due process required that once they had started an inquiry, it had to be completed. The battle lines were drawn. The first stop was with the police chief.

"I know these two well, along with that minister, and let me tell you, I have had enough of them, Mel. I am going to assign some of my best detectives to this case. As a suggestion, you might apply to the courts, in the meantime, to have that ridiculous law struck down!"

# Chapter 34

The uniformed police officers stood before the door of the Spiritual Center, feeling a little ridiculous as they knocked.

"We are sorry to bother you, however, they have given us orders to present your business with a Cease and Desist Order. We also need to take possession of all relevant documents, so we will need to have access to your office and files."

As they walked in, they could smell the wonderful scent of bread baking. They knew they were going to struggle, keeping themselves focused. Every person they passed as they walked to the office smiled at them and wished them a great day.

By the time they had walked to the office, the police officers had pretty well forgotten why they had come to the center.

"Do you have time for some fresh baked bread and some wonderful, sweet tea?" asked a member. "You can come sit with us in our cafeteria, if you like. Please feel free to speak with any of the members seated there."

Even though they knew they were breaking regulations, the officers headed for the cafeteria. They needed no coaxing. As they sat down, a staff member placed an enormous plate of baked bread just out of the oven, covered with butter and strawberry jam before them. And that tea! They had never had tea that was so delicious before.

Before long, the officers were happily playing yoga with their new friends. The reason for their visit was long forgotten.

On the way back to headquarters, they felt a little embarrassed that they had chosen not to fulfill their duties on this project, however, when they had reported to the chief, they realized that every officer who had shared the same assignment was sitting in the roll call room... with the same expression on their face.

"Did you leave the Cease and Desist Orders at each site?" asked the chief of each officer. "If you did, that is all we can expect for today." The chief would punish none of the officers for not carrying out the task, as he hoped they would fail.

Late that night, he ordered other officers to place padlocks on the front entrances of each of the centers with the Cease and Desist order pasted to the doors.

The following morning, he ordered officers to drive by to ensure the order was being complied with, but became concerned when several hours later, none of them had reported back.

He jumped into his car to check out the site nearest the HQ. When he arrived, all the members were on the lawn doing the Downward Dog... and so were his officers!

Not making a noise, he found a spot and joined them!

During the closing meditation, he felt the urge to open his eyes to look at the person beside him. Mike smiled and waved at him. The chief recalled his visit with Mike that day of the riots as he closed his eyes, returning to his happy place in the quiet.

When he opened his eyes, there was no one beside him, just a vacant spot on the grass.

––––––––––––––––

A few days later, the minister stopped by to speak to the police chief. It was his poor timing that he arrived as he entered the office as the chief was in the midst of completing a cobra yoga pose on the floor behind his desk.

"Don't tell me they got you now too! Did the orders get served to all the sites, Chief? Is there anyone around here who is still sane?"

Chief nodded at him smiling, then moved into a Cat and Dog pose. The minister shook his head, feeling he was the only sane person left in the world. He then walked away, shaking his head.

His next stop was at his lawyer friend's office. He found it locked up with a handwritten notice tacked onto the door. "Gone on vacation. Back when I get back."

Minister did not know that both the lawyer and the judge had a visitor during a recent sleep. Of course, we know who it was, but can you guess what happened when Guardian Angel Rachel spoke with them?

Well, they both decided that things had gotten too crazy for them at home, so they packed their bags and their bank accounts and moved very far away.

It was not a well-planned event, so things went a little awry. Within a week of finding their new home, they were both relieved of their money by a local entrepreneur, so they would not need to have concerns about it anymore.

And since they were now residing in a foreign jurisdiction, they could not practice their professions. They now got to live as street people since they had no job or money and could not afford to go home. Justice was served!

So, is the minister getting away scot-free through all this business?

Well, he was beginning to think so, but no.

Behind his back, all the ministers of his churches were now getting quite good at practicing yoga!

They had filed a class-action lawsuit against him, claiming he had defrauded their churches for a great deal of money. They then filed a lien against their church building as an individual, so that when the suit was settled, they would each own the building.

When he received all the summons, the minister was outraged! How dare they? Those were his churches!

That night he set out in the dark, intending to burn down all twelve of them. However, he received second-degree burns to his hand trying to set fire to the first one and had to go to the hospital. The building was fine.

Camping was not his strong suit, I would say!

When the police chief heard of his nocturnal escapade the next morning, he charged him with arson. The crown prosecutor, who now also practiced yoga, saw the writ and had the case heard tout-suite.

Within only a couple of months, the head minister had no head anymore, the lawyer and the judge were street people in a foreign land, the church ministers all owned their own buildings where they joined in with the yoga craze and all the police force (although they kept their jobs) spent most of their time doing yoga since no one was committing any crimes. Cool, eh!

# Chapter 35

The Hundred Monkey Syndrome had proven itself. Everyday life had begun to change. Even folks who had chosen not to take part in the Spiritual Centers were feeling different. They could not explain why they felt different... but they did.

The usual became very different. People gathered in parks to visit with each other, instead of bars. Picnics and campouts became the norm. People found new trails to explore and breathed in nature's beauty.

Instead of smoking cigarettes or using drugs, they smelled roses, honeysuckle, and phlox while they picked fruit from their trees.

People were more relaxed, finding they needn't push against life anymore.

They found with the reduced stress; they enjoyed eating a lighter fare. One result of this change was the market for heavy meats declined. As a result, the animal farmers transitioned their operations to coincide with the change in appetite.

This was not the end of the transitions by any stretch!

Many fields dedicated to animal husbandry were turned back to nature. Flowers and medicinal herbs blossomed in the old manure. Honey bees flourished to assist Mother Nature by toting pollen from flower to flower. Nature was in its glory. Everything became calm.

The world was beginning to look the way Mother Earth had intended!

So, how about the people themselves? Let's hope they did more than stop smoking cigarettes! Could they have grasped more than just reconnecting with nature?

Signs were abounding that the spiritual evolution of human beings had kicked into a higher gear. An interpreter was no longer needed to understand higher truths. People could access and study them for themselves.

As each person became more aware, they learned that the way they feel at any time is an indicator of an issue in their life at that moment. The sensation would lead them to a new level of personal truth, which helped them to be more self-responsible. They learned to choose how to react to their immediate situation by choice. They learned to not repeat old habits that made their lives miserable. The attainment of inner joy became the guiding force.

The evolution expanded more and more as people became more aware. Soon, they learned that by dealing with their misunderstandings; they attained better health... and more personal freedom.

Reverend Harry was a happy man. His flock now counted in the millions. He led workshops on spiritual evolution in the home center. He needed to do this to maintain his connection with the people. Now that he knew his true place in life, he set the activities of his day-to-day life up to ensure he kept that connection strong. The demands of the administration side would not derail his authentic place. Besides, his flock would not hear of it either. They still loved their Reverend Harry.

Harry's next class was going to be an interesting one. He hoped it would make space for another new level of clearing that could help millions of people. This class would focus on the various levels of karma.

"To understand karma, we must break it down. The simplest way to explain this amazing force is to call it the law of cause and effect.

We are here today to examine this Universal force in its various levels. They are personal, family, and social.

Our goal is to understand how Karma works in our lives. We will also look at how it has worked in our genetic history since time immemorial. We can then restructure the limiting memories we carry within us, most of which we are not even aware of."

Harry paused for a moment to allow his class to digest the introduction.

"When scientists speak of genetic history or DNA, they are often referring to karmic history. Repeated or traumatic emotional events whose memories we store in the cells of the body create the DNA. If we do not clear this history, we pass it on to descending generations. This does not mean that all DNA is created this way. It only refers to the genetics of beliefs.

Even in the Bible, there is reference to this. It is stated that it takes several generations to clear the acts of one person who caused trauma to another. This is very evident in cases of violence and sexual abuse."

"So you are not talking about hair or skin color or height, etc., Reverend Harry?" asked one attendee.

"Almost correct, John. Hair and skin color are correct, but there could be a correlation regarding height. The Pituitary gland manages height in the body. If there is a trauma created that impacts the function of this gland, it could affect a person's height."

"What would be an example of a karmic reaction that would affect other generations of folks?" asked another.

"The trauma evoked by wars is a stark example. The terror caused by the violations to the human spirit provoked intense fear, shaking the human emotions to the core. These emotional reactions to such catastrophic events create karmic memory.

Historical events such as war, slavery, mass illnesses, and mass starvation all create this type of memory. The cellular storage of these traumas is often not even recognized by modern medical practices as a part of each person's lineage or as a cause of certain health issues.

Until these events are cleared, and we choose to take a different path, they will repeat themselves again and again. We need to rethink our perspective on them. They are not an untreatable part of our consciousness. They are not just a part of our history. They continue living in our own DNA today.

Left unrecognized, these memories limit the evolution of the soul. The ego carries the memory in the subconscious. They create an ongoing limitation in the person's life that affects their self-expression.

In previous sessions, we have been dealing with personal karma, even though we may not have called it such. Today's topic is family and social karma. We will group them together since they both relate to memories that affect groups of people and have evolved from their genetic lineage."

John asked, "So, are you saying that the struggles my great grandparents may have had in their lives trying to survive have impacted me, and maybe even my children?"

"If the impact either lasted for long periods or they were traumatic enough, absolutely. If they emigrated from another country, they started their new lives from nothing. Since they had to work to find somewhere to live, find food, and build their new home, there is going to be cellular memory of the trials and tribulations they endured. This was not an easy process for them! One did not pop into the local welfare office for financial support or to get a hotel room. They literally started from nothing. It took them years to develop any level of comfort, if they ever did.

So, there are two aspects to be recognized today. The first, we are already speaking about. That is the events of our forebears. Just as important are the traumatic events that each of us, as individuals, endured. The trauma that is occurring in our present lives may be correlated with ancestral events.

In order to get clear, these issues have to be recognized and reframed. Most people do not realize that these issues affect them in their daily lives by tainting their perspective of life's abundance. Can anyone give me some examples?"

This class was exploding with excitement. The attendees yelled out answers as they thought of them.

"Physical violence."

"Sexual violence."

"Going hungry."

"Being abandoned."

"Not feeling safe."

"Favoritism amongst siblings."

They just kept yelling them out. There were so many answers. Harry smiled to himself and waited until they were done.

"You guys are fantastic! Every answer is correct... and correctable. This will be the focus of this workshop."

It was becoming very clear that these people understood there was still a lot of work to be done. Humans have inhabited this planet for over 15,000 years this time around. That meant there was 15000 years of unconscious training to undo. This project would take some special input.

# Chapter 36

The members of the Wind Surfers sat on the lawn of the original spiritual center, along with Harry, Rose, Frank, and Mel.

As they enjoyed the quiet time, they chatted, reminiscing about the changes in recent days. Ever so quietly, they were joined by Rachel, Oona, and Tan.

No one had noticed the three newcomers, so when Rachel spoke, they were shaken back into the real world. She began:

*"The lives of human beings have improved so much through everyone's contributions. So many, many people have begun living in their truth and growing from the inside.*

*There is much more work to be done to integrate solid and permanent change at higher levels. However, for now, it is important to support them in taking the time to embrace and integrate these profound changes into their lives.*

*Mother Earth is breathing so much more easily now that so many humans have realized that living in accordance with nature is much healthier than trying to overcome or eradicate the very forces that support their own existence.*

*As always, in the process of evolution, life may seem perfect now compared to the ways of the past. However, the evolution has just begun. It is our job to continue to lead the way and keep it going. There is so much more to life than we can know. The route to knowing is the path of Ascension.*

*In the meantime, there is space for us to just enjoy life, whether by taking part in some of our favorite activities or through any projects that come forward, so please enjoy, as always. After all, this is why we incarnated in this now... to love life, to be thankful for our lives, and to enjoy each moment, no matter what.*

*Blessings to each of you."*

And at that Rachel, Oona and Tan rode off on their motorcycles... vintage black Harley-Davidsons!

## Would you like a
## free visualization video?

As a thank you for purchasing and reading my book, I would like to gift you with a free video.

This video is not just for entertainment, it is a video that shows you a technique for managing stress and anxiety.

Just click this link to join my email list and the video will magically appear in your email.

My promise to you is that I hold your email sacred and will only use it to connect with you myself.

Here is a sneak peek of Book 3

# Chapter 1

"Everything looks so beautiful! The plants are so shiny, they are almost hard to look at."

"It is what happens when people care, my dear. Nature loves to give back like this. It is a natural connection."

Dawn and one of the other members were walking through the gardens, chatting. It was another wonderful day in Greenwood Commons.

"I guess we should find our way back. The meeting this morning is about our new children's program. This should be exciting too."

"I would never have believed that life could be so good. If you had asked me a couple of years ago when everything was barren and all the people were so angry, I would have thought this was an impossible dream. We sure have to be thankful for those folks who got rid of all that bad energy. I wonder whatever happened to them."

"My feeling is they are still around here somewhere, watching us. Reverend Harry has sure developed an amazing relationship with them."

"And he grew so much, too. He is so much more now. It seems you just touch him now and whatever is bothering you, disappears. Do you think this is what it was like when Master Jesus walked the earth?"

"I think so. It is so nice to be able to reach out to him, then watch the changes happen. Much of what we have been looking at during our walk today was his doing. We can often see him sitting on one of our park benches, looking like he is meditating. My suspicion is, he is chatting with the plant divas. Every time he does, whatever he is doing, the plants seem shinier, and they are so fragrant. Even plants I have never smelled before emit a beautiful perfume."

They entered the cafeteria as everyone was settling in, since the meeting was about to start. A typical Saturday morning!

Since Greenwood Commons was a cohousing community, every resident was a board member.

Decisions were made by consensus, and not until it was attained. It was fortunate, the game players had long been weeded out, so the meetings always flowed well. Each person attending wanted the best for everyone.

It was Dawn's turn to lead the meeting this day since the focus was on the new children's gardening program.

"Good morning, my friends. It is my pleasure to lead this meeting this morning. We have some exciting new projects to begin now that spring is well underway.

Let's take a few moments to tune into the energies, so we all provide the best input into this session."

They had all done this process a hundred times, so it did not take long for the energies to rise to a suitable level. As they focused on their breaths, taking long slow breaths, moving their bellies to draw in the most air possible, they visualized gold energy emitting from their solar plexuses. The energy swirled through the room, joining the energies of all the others.

The combined energy spread wide and far, reaching beyond the room, out into the gardens, throughout the town, the region, even reaching right out to the Cosmos.

Connecting with Source always felt so good!

As everyone returned, smiles so huge, they almost cracked the owner's face radiated throughout.

"The focus of today's meeting is on helping our children connect with the plant energies so they can learn to understand their relationship with nature itself.

My suggestion is that we build planter boxes in the patio area for raised box gardening. This will make it easy for the children to see how their gardens are growing rather than just letting them take part in looking after the bigger gardens."

One member jumped in right away, adding, "I knew this was your plan, so I took the liberty of ordering the material from our board manufacturing plant. This way, we can get right to the work party this morning."

Another member added, "I have placed several wheel barrels of soil nearby. We should be able to have these boxes ready to plant this afternoon."

"Well, what are we sitting here for? Let's get to it. Meeting adjourned if all agree." Dawn was the first out the door.

Younger families comprised most of the people living in this community. Ever since the ordeal with the orb and all its offspring had been resolved, the birthrate had skyrocketed in this town.

Everyone had found peace here as positive energy flowed into every situation. Reverend Harry still offered programs for personal evolution at the center. Teesha was still busy with her myriad of yoga classes, too. It was easy to feel the love!

The town's economic health had soon been restored too when the Windsurfers arrived with their plans for the board plant. Who would have ever thought that a town could thrive on helping Mother Earth! Collecting and repurposing all the garbage plastic that was destined to be dumped into the waste stream (or trout streams) had saved the day.

Trucks arrived daily with loads of plastic. As quick as a wink, it was melted, mixed with sawdust or whatever other former waste was available. Then, the mixture was turned into building boards of any shape and size desired.

This day's lumber has been created by laying many layers of strips of cardboard throughout the length of the mold. Adding the natural dye to the mixture made it almost impossible to tell these boards from the old ones made from cutting down and destroying trees. They would make great planter boxes!

---

The building party stood outside, assessing the location where the planters would live. Of course, there were plenty of yummy treats and drinks to fuel the workers.

Inclusion of the children was important to the adults since this project was for them. Defining their jobs came first. There were ten large planter boxes and six small planters for smaller plants, like herbs. The parents let the children choose which they were moved to help with.

In a flash, there were many busy little beavers. Children could see what needed to be done. Soon, the parents found themselves in advisory roles as the children let their engineering skills come to life.

The younger children placed the bases where the planters would reside. Next, they helped put the side boards in place as the older children screwed and nailed each container together.

It only took a couple of hours for the project to be completed. All that needed to be done now was add the soil. (The children thought this would be a nice job for the parents since they needed refreshments after such hard work!)

As the planting began, Dawn had the children stand around her. She explained the importance of creating the gardens.

"It is very important for us to know each of the plants. We need to know its name, why we are planting it, and who its friends are. Plants, like humans, need to share their lives with others who support them. They also need to be placed where the environment is suitable for their ability to thrive.

In these smaller boxes, we are going to plant herbs. Do you know why we like to grow lots of different kinds of herbs? Anyone?"

Right away, the answers rang out. "Making supper yummy." "Making soaps." "Making the air smell nice." Everyone laughed and laughed. This was another good day.

"Now when we plant, remember to give loving energy to the soil, to the plants and, to the environment surrounding. As we become one with the plants, they feel the love. This makes them want to grow nice and healthy. When they are ready, they will taste so much better than plants that are not treated special.

Every day, we must come to visit them and share our energy by focusing on them. We must also energize the water before we bless them with it."

The children all stood in front of the planter they had helped construct. As they placed their hands over the containers, they projected gold energy to the soil and to the plants. They focused in their minds on how much they loved their friends in nature.

It was easy to see the plants respond to this loving attention. There would be some yummy veggies soon!!!

# Chapter 2

**"**What are you doing my dear?"

Suzie was standing looking into the fish pond. It was a cute little pond only about four feet round. She had a funny look on her face as her dad walked up to her.

"I am talking to the man." Suzie pointed at the pond as she said it.

"Really, there is a man in the pond, Suzie? What is he doing?" Dad was not sure what antics his daughter was up to this time. He knew she had quite an imagination and liked making up stories, but he was aware enough that he did not want to make her stop telling her stories. Some of them were quite fanciful, but what child doesn't have imaginary friends or Unicorns at some point in their young lives?

"He is real daddy. He was talking to me. Honest. He told me to tell you that everyone needed to be careful. Situations are developing that might cause us problems if we do not pay heed. What does heed mean daddy?"

## About The Author

I hope you are having fun with this story. I also hope that you are learning concepts and tools that, at least, spark conversations focused on the future of mankind.

I have dedicated my life to the mystic's way. For over 50 years now I have pursued esoteric knowledge through my membership in the Rosicrucian Order AMORC as well as studying and practicing esoteric modalities such as Reiki, Jin Shin Jyutsu, Core Belief Engineering, Heart Resonance Therapy, and probably many others. So many, I have forgotten some of them by now.

It all started though when I attended Douglas College in New Westminster BC. There I enrolled in a program called Human Development. This program cleverly created by two social workers revealed the world of the unconscious mind. As I learned about core beliefs, I also started seeing people's energies. I found I could read people's auras, extracting information that helped them understand the aspects of their mind that held them back.

If you are interested in learning more about the esoteric side of life and how understanding the unseen will help you live more fully, then please check out my Facebook page and my YouTube channels, both called Powerful You Powerful Me.

The more we understand and accept the invisible side of ourselves, the more powerful we are as people. Only by helping others grow, do we really grow ourselves as long as it is carried out in honor and respect.

**Join my Facebook Group and YouTube Channel**

The story of the Ascenders Return To Grace is only the start!

We are in the most tumultuous times man has known in this cycle. As we move deeper into the cusp between Pisces and Aquarius (what the Christians call Armageddon), there is so much opportunity for each of us to grow at a soul level.

The dark energies are running amok on our planet. We have a choice, whether we choose to accept it or not. Either we succumb to the egocentric lifestyles of the dark side, or we choose to live in the light of the Universe.

This is not a religious-based choice. It is a choice of whether or not you choose to evolve as a human being.

Through my Facebook group and the YouTube channels, you will be able to communicate with me and other folks who are thought leaders in this mindset. You will also be invited to learn various tools for managing your mind and your life so you can live a more fulfilling expression of yourself.

It is truly through the energy of Universal Love that we exist and prosper. Now is the time to come to the light.

You can also join my fan base by clicking on the link below. I promise to only contact you with relevant information that will help you to express the amazing person you truly are.

In appreciation of your trusting me, I will send you a video of a mind management visualization I channeled that will get you started. It will help you manage those pesky thoughts that roam around in your head wreaking havoc.

A clear, peaceful mind is good, and the true path to Ascension.

**Facebook Group link**

Powerful You Powerful Me[1]

**Monty's Website**

www.powerfulyoupowerfulme.com

---

## Acknowledgments

It is with a humble heart I thank Judith Hunter, once again for being my eyes. Without her astute perceptions, this document could never have become the shiny polished story it stands as today.

I also raise a hand in appreciation to all the folks at the Self-Publishing School for their encouragement and training that has helped me become a professional writer.

And lastly, but most special, thanks to my Guardian Angel Rachel for her input in creating this story. Could not have done it without you!

**Books by Monty C. Ritchings**
**Available on any online book store**
**Embracing The Blend**
What Mom and Dad Didn't Know They Were

  Teaching You

**Stamp Out Stress**
Living With Stress is a Choice, Not a Fact of Life
**Chakras Demystified**
Our True Communication System Revealed!
**Healthy Children Only Need Three Things**
**The Ascenders Return To Grace Books**
**Let's Get Hiking**
The Essential Guide for Serious Hikers and
Walkers